rock

anyta Sunday

First published in 2014 by Anyta Sunday,
Contact at Buerogemeinschaft ATP24, Am Treptower Park 24, 12435 Berlin,
Germany

An Anyta Sunday publication
www.anytasunday.com

Cover Design Natasha Snow

Content Editor: *Teresa Crawford*
Line Editor: *HJS Editing*
Proof Editor: *Lynda Lamb*

This book contains sexual content.

For all the rocks out there . . .

~~This is the story of how I fall in love.~~
~~This is the story of how my home breaks and is rebuilt.~~

This is the story of how I became a rock.

part one: igneous

igneous: of and pertaining to fire.

gabbro

New day, new stone.

Today's is a small trapezium of coarse-grained gabbro that's spilling through the fence of our neighbor's yard. I squat to pick up the grey-black stone, jumping when a fresh raindrop slides across it and splashes onto my wrist. I squeeze the stone. Stone 3621.

The gabbro's subtle weight increases as I tell it all the crap that happened today, my last day of intermediate school. Nothing dramatic, just saying goodbye to my teachers and high-fiving my mates going to St. Patrick's and Scott's College next year.

I drop the stone into my pocket and breathe in the perfumed air rising from the magnolias that flank the street. Today smells different, like the cusp of summer.

Home looms before me, and I swing my backpack off before peeking into the letterbox. Emptied already. I fling our gate open. Its squeals match the rickety fence and clumps of wildflowers I trample as I walk across the front lawn. Ivy climbs the wooden pillars that support the veranda roof and give our home a cottage-like look. Small and cozy.

Except something is off. The door is held open by a faded kitchen-appliance box and—

A high-pitched gurgle. I quicken my steps toward the sound.

My older sister Annie is sitting at the end of the veranda, huddled against the side of the house in a crimson sundress, head bowed into her hands.

"Annie?" I drop my backpack onto the cracked brick path. Annie's tears drop onto her Roman sandals. "What happened?" I crouch and grab her knees.

Her green eyes resemble mine, flecked with hazel, one ever so slightly brighter than the other. Enough to make strangers look twice.

Except now, as Annie blinks, she looks different. The skin around her eyes is swollen and red, and the mascara she's not allowed to wear weaves complicated webs over her cheeks.

Her mouth opens and shuts, and another sob rattles her. I don't know what to do. She's my big sis; she's usually the one comforting *me.*

I pat her shoulder. She rests her head against my arm, smudging her black tears across my skin. It tickles, but I shake it off. "Did . . ." I swallow. "Did someone die?"

She shakes her head and relief sweetens my next gulp of air. I rock back on my feet. So long as no one is dead, I can handle anything. Maybe her first boyfriend dumped her? Two days before her fourteenth birthday, though? I'm only twelve, but getting dumped like that would have to suck.

Annie sniffs hard, as if trying to regain control. She wipes her tears, drawing the mascara outward so it resembles cat whiskers.

"Our home is breaking, Cooper," she says. All thoughts of cats flee my mind.

The appliance box that's propping the front door open takes on a new significance. "What do you mean?" I ask. But I already know.

My sister's voice grows taut, strangled and angry. "It means a week here, a week there. It means choosing Mum's side or Dad's. It means we have a *new* family."

I don't understand this last part; in fact, I can't quite grip the first part either.

Clouds pass over the afternoon sun, and the veranda darkens like a bad omen.

"They're getting a divorce?" It comes out like a question, but it isn't. Of *course* that's what she means. They're getting a divorce.

"It's more than that." Annie glares at me. "Dad has someone else. Do you understand? He has this whole other life we don't know about. He wants to move in with *her*, because *she*'s the real love of his life. All those business trips? It was him being with her. With *them*."

My breath comes in and out fast. I'm not sure I want more details, but I ask anyway. "Them?" This can't be real. Sure, Dad leaves for two weeks out of the month, but he always brings back gifts for us. Always says he loves us to the moon and back. "Them?" I ask firmly.

"The bitch has a son and is pregnant."

I flinch. "A son? Dad's?" Our . . . brother?

"The son isn't his, but the baby—" Her voice breaks. "I'm staying with Mum. I don't want anything to do with him. I hate him."

Footsteps creak over the wooden boards. I don't know how long Dad's been standing there, but his expression is tight and pain flashes in his gaze—green like ours. We are our father's children.

But for how much longer?

Dad folds his arms across his old, oil-smeared shirt. He's fit for thirty-eight, but the creased skin around his eyes can't be denied. I'd like to believe that his crow's feet came from endless smiles, but all I ever see are frowns.

I guess the smiling must have happened when he was with *her*. With *them*.

Dad looks from Annie to me, and his sad frown hits me like a punch to my gut. I can't breathe.

"Cooper," he says. It comes out raspy, like he's been crying. "Cooper," he pleas.

I glance from Annie to Dad, feeling like I have to choose. My breathing quickens and I need my stone. Like, right now. I plunge my hand into my pocket and strangle this bad memory into the gabbro. I look at Annie. At Dad.

Choose! Choose! Choose!

But I can't.

basalt

Mum begs me to spend the weekend with Dad. She stands tall and fair, with freckles that I didn't inherit—save the ones on my toe and under my eye—as she pulls out T-shirts, shorts, and socks from my dresser drawers. I hurry over to take care of my own boxer shorts, thank you very much.

She pauses, arms full of clothes that are ready to collect her tears, but she holds back. I'm not fooled by the façade of strength.

I understand why Annie wants to take sides; why she chose Mum's.

"We were both to blame. Things haven't been working out for a long time," she says with a smile far too bright to be real. "Don't be as stubborn as your sister. It hurts him, not seeing you."

"It's only been a month."

"He's called every second day."

"He left *you*, right? So he chose this." But those are Annie's words, not mine, and I feel guilty for saying them.

"He left, but we were already broken."

"Have you met his new . . . woman?" I ask, for lack of a better word—and because it sounds rude and mean, and I want to spite her.

She pauses and unzips my duffel bag with a swift flick of her wrist. "Yes." She looks away, but not before I see tears finally rimming her eyes. "Lila was once a friend of mine. We've known each other since our first day of university. In fact, she introduced me to your father."

She packs my bags even though I can easily do it myself. But she needs something to keep her busy, so I let her. She tosses in my journal, throws in last week's collection of stones, and places my magnifying glass between piles of clothes.

"I'm sorry," I say.

She shakes her head. "I'll be okay, Cooper. You'll see."

Mum drops me off outside Dad's house. The worst part of going to Dad's is how close it is to Mum's. I'd always thought Dad was in Auckland the weeks he wasn't with us, but his other life had been only a few neighborhoods over the whole time.

How long? I asked Dad that day on the veranda. When he didn't answer, I shouted. *How long?*

"Guess this is it, then," I say. Mum glances toward his house—his *mansion.*

Château de Dad has a large, freshly-mowed lawn that glints in the mid-morning light so that the grass glimmers like a moat. Except this castle is modern, all straight lines and glass, and crowned by a hilly forest in the distance. It makes a simple, powerful statement: *We're better than you.*

I understand why Mum looks away.

I want to lean over and hug her, but Mum isn't the hugging type. Instead, I shrink into my seat and refuse to unbuckle my seatbelt.

Maybe this weekend isn't such a great idea after all.

"We can go back home," I say, running a hand through my messy locks as if I'm trying to be like *them*, trying to prove I'm just as good even though I'm not the one Dad chose. "I wish Annie was coming."

"She'll get there, sooner or later." Mum grips the wheel like she's ready to leave. "She needs more time to adjust."

I don't tell her maybe I need that time too. She's counting on me to be the peace offering; to show that she is all fine and dandy with this. Like she wants to prove that she's the reasonable, accepting one. Like she wants Dad to know that nothing can get to her, and that she's not turning us against him. She's no bitch. She's gracious. Tolerant. Accepting. She wants to rub what he's thrown away in his face.

And I want to give that to her.

But I am nervous, and my belly is lurching like it needs food, even though that's the last thing I want. I rub my sweaty palms over my shorts and grab the duffel bag between my feet, hauling it onto my lap. "It's only the weekend."

"Just the weekend," she repeats. Something in her monotonous tone makes me shiver. Does she think because it's a mansion I won't come home?

I don't care that she doesn't like hugs; I give her one anyway. The angle is awkward and her short hair finds its way up my nose. Even though she doesn't hug back, she warms me inside and out. "Love you." I draw away and finally undo my seatbelt.

"I was young," she says, "when I met your father. I thought we were in love."

I fumble to open the door. A rush of sweet summer air washes into the car. Mum snaps out of her reverie and laughs. "Whatever you do, Cooper, don't fall—I hope it's different for you and Annie."

pumice

I walk to the front porch through the moat instead of on the path. I dig my heels in a bit too, hoping to make my stride look clumpy and ripe with attitude. I dump my duffel bag on the porch and ring the bell. When no one answers, I check the windows.

A familiar yell comes from the distance; it's my dad's voice, but it's attached to laughter. My spirits fall to the freckle on my large toe. I kick at the skirting of the house but it does nothing except make my foot throb. "Shit!" I hop around to the side of the house and stop in the shadows.

My dad is kicking a soccer ball to a boy whose back is to me. The boy has short brown hair and skin that's seen some sun, judging by the tan. The way he moves forward to meet the ball with a precise, hefty kick suggests he's the cocky type who knows he's good and flaunts it.

With a grin, Dad catches the ball on his knee and heads it. He lets it fall behind him, using his heel to kick it over to the front again. He passes it back to the boy. "Try that on for size."

The boy sniggers and repeats the juggling without a slip. He smoothly kicks the ball back. "Give me a real challenge, Dad."

I must not have heard him right. I shake my head. *Dad?*

I wait for Dad to correct him, to remind this presumptuous boy that he should call him David, not Dad. But he doesn't. He smiles.

My vision blurs with angry tears. He's *my* dad. How dare this cocky dickweed call him that! Cold fury fills me, and I stalk out from behind the side of the house.

Dad sees me first. His kick misfires, and the ball hurtles toward me. Dad looks suddenly nervous, then excited, and then nervous again as he glances from the boy to me.

I stop the ball right before the boy turns around.

A breeze makes the trees in the hills shiver, while the sun brightens. The heat soaks into my skin and sweat drips down my back.

I stare at him. He's older than me, maybe my sister's age. He's tall, teetering on the edge of lankiness, like he's a few summers off from growing into his build. His lips are curved into a half grin, confirming my suspicions. Cocky, like we've started a game that he knows he's going to win. He glances over at my dad, then turns his blue eyes on me. They are the blue of the rubbish bags Mum uses for the bathroom bin; the blue of oily seawater; the blue of regurgitated fish scales.

"Cooper," Dad says, waving me closer. "You're here early."

I glare at the boy, who doesn't appear intimidated or nervous. In fact, his smile might be growing. "Gonna pass the ball or what?" he asks. He chuckles and taps a fist against his chest. "I'm Jace, by the way."

Jace? What type of name is that?

A nice one.

I hate it.

Tears blur my vision. Dad knows this boy, knows Jace. Knows him like a . . .

I stare at the soccer ball at my feet. I move my foot back, aligning it perfectly. If Jace thinks he's the only one who's good with a ball, he's wrong. I kick hard and whisper, "Heads up."

The ball smacks him in the face as he's turning.

"Fuck!" His garbled words spill out as he clutches his nose. "What the hell?" He spits onto the grass and I proudly note the blood.

I want to give myself a high-five, but the gleam in his

regurgitated fish-scale eyes changes my mind. I start forward, apologies on the tip of my tongue. Maybe I wish I hadn't done it. Maybe.

He stares hard at me. The cockiness is gone, replaced with something colder and more calculating. I have a feeling he's going to remember every detail of this moment for the rest of his life.

Dad hollers something about brothers, but his voice softens as if he pities me.

I stare at my Puma shoes, fascinated by the slowly-unraveling double knots and dirt clods clumped into the sole.

Jace wipes away the tiny trail of blood seeping from his nose. When he speaks, his words crawl across my skin and give me goose bumps.

"Well, Dad," he says tightly, "isn't this the brother I've always wanted?"

* * *

Jace plants himself onto the kitchen counter and slaps an ice pack against his face.

"Fucker," he mutters, scowling at me.

"Dickweed," I retort. I'm sitting at the large dining table scowling back.

"Cooper." Dad slaps his palm onto my shoulder. "This is not how I wanted you two to start."

"Start? Start what?"

Dad answers, "Our new life."

He says more but I can't hear the words. His voice drones and hurts my head. "I hate you." This time they are not my sister's words. They're all mine. "Five years? Five?" My voice breaks. "How could you? I'll never forgive you."

My chair protests with a squeal as I push it back and stand. I turn my back to them and rush away, refusing to run, though my blood is pumping like it's chanting for me to run. But I can't because . . . because . . .

Because I want dad to pull me into a hug and tell me this

is all a joke, all a mistake, and he's coming home. I'd settle for him telling me that Annie and I are just as good as his new family—but if that were true, he never would have left us.

I grab my duffel bag and march over the grassy moat to the street. I have some loose change in my pocket, so I head toward the bus stop and search the sidewalk for a stone. Preferably something sharp, something *broken*. A cracked corner of the gutter catches my eye.

Concrete is made of rock, sand, and gravel—sometimes even pumice for the lightweight stuff. It'd have to do.

I kick a wedge of it loose and try to stuff it into my pocket. A hand grabs my arm and pulls me around.

My heart lifts, and I almost drop the concrete. "Dad." I turn to face him.

Except it's Jace.

I have to raise my chin to look at him. A frown cuts across his brow. He loosens his grip on me, but he doesn't let go until I pointedly glance at his hand.

"You're still a shit," he says. His voice softens. "It sucks. I mean it *really* sucks. Like raw nerves and lemon juice and"—he looks over his shoulder—"I always wondered who you were."

The duffel bag handles are cutting into one of my palms, and the jagged rock is scraping the other. I clutch them tightly as I think how to respond. He always wondered? Always? But that must mean—"You knew about us?"

Jace takes the duffel bag from my grasp. "Just come back to the house," he says with a quizzical glance to the rock in my hand. I push the stone deep into my pocket, ripping the seams a little. "If not for Dad, then for answers to your questions."

I might have gone had he not said *Dad*, but that one word catapults me back toward the bus stop. Jace can have my stupid duffel bag. I don't care. I'll be all right. I have my rock. "Tell him he can visit me, but I'm never coming back here again."

tuff

Dad stops by to visit me and Annie, but my sister refuses to see him. Dad settles on taking me for a walk through the town belt. For three hours we hike the hills and weave through the woods in the crisp air. Birds tweet like they're gossiping about us.

They don't talk much these two, do they?

The smaller one looks like he's swallowed sour worms, poor thing.

What about the taller one? He looks one peck of the beak away from crying.

They need to talk.

How can we make them?

Sparrow, are you fully digested yet?

Aim. Load. Fire—

Bird shit lands on my cap. "Gross!" I yank the cap off.

Dad chuckles and takes care of it. "There, all gone." He hands it back to me and I reluctantly slip it on again. "It's good luck you know."

"Really? Will it make you come home again?"

Dad sighs and sits on a bench, patting the space next to him. "I'm sorry things are hard for you and Annie."

"Do you love her? Is she really your true love? Did you ever care for Mum?"

"Your mum and I have a complicated history."

"What does that mean?"

"It means we were on again, off again when we first got together. She's got a wonderful spirit, your mum, and we cared for each other a lot—"

"But?"

"Relationships don't always work. Fifteen years ago, I thought we were broken up for good."

"Why'd you get back together then?"

"Three or four months after we broke up, she brought me the news that she was pregnant. I cared about her, Cooper. I wanted to do the right thing."

"So you had a shot-gun wedding, and the baby came early?"

Dad frowns. "Everyone knew about the baby already. Annie came out on time. Her tiny, red hands gripped my finger so tightly, I knew she needed me. She needed her father, and I wanted to be the best I could for her. It worked for a time after that. Your mum and me, I mean. We had a routine and we both loved Annie so much, and we'd laugh at each other when we were too tired to do anything else. And then, Annie was about six months old when your mum got pregnant again."

"Ever heard of contraception?" I ask, although I'm not too mad at his lack of foresight, considering I came into the world and all. But still.

"She was on the mini-pill. We thought we were good."

"So I was a mistake?"

"Cooper, when I found out your mum was pregnant, all I could think was how much I loved your sister and how happy I was she'd have a sibling."

"So what happened? When did it all go downhill?"

"It wasn't working." He sighs and shakes his head. "We were fooling ourselves."

"Got it," I say, jumping up from the bench. "Then you met *her* and realized *she* was the love of your life. You decide to cheat on Mum for five years, and *boom*, now it's all blowing up in your face. Well it's tuff, isn't it?" *Tuff.* The debris from a volcanic eruption.

This whole situation is his mess. *He* will have to clean it up.

Dad scrambles after me. "Cooper, wait. It didn't work out how we hoped, but I didn't go behind your mother's back—"

"Her son starts calling you *Dad*, and you just go with it?"

"Cooper, wait—"

I raise a hand. "I don't want to hear any more."

obsidian

The first weeks at Newtown High go by quickly. I attend classes, do my homework, and even make a couple of friends—aptly nicknamed Ernie and Bert for their size difference and close friendship.

The first months with separated parents drag. Dad keeps calling, I keep ignoring. Annie does the same, and her skirts have all shrunk a couple of sizes.

We're in desperate need of black obsidian to ward off our negativity.

Beginning of the third week of school, the phone rings.

Mum waits four counts, willing me or Annie to step up to the plate. We don't bite.

She sighs and answers the phone. "David," she says tightly. "The kids still need a bit of time—" Mum frowns and twists her back to us. "Oh, David. I'm sorry to hear that. Will she be okay?"

Annie and I, sharing a couch, shuffle forward. I tense, waiting for what Mum will say next. Even Annie is gripping the arm of the couch.

Did Dad call to say he made a mistake? Is he coming home?

I hold my breath as Mum glances at us. "Yes. I'll tell them. Take care." She hangs up.

She sits on the armchair across from our couch, her mouth set in a grim line. She leans forward and clasps her fingers.

“That was your dad with some sad news. Lila lost her baby.”

“How far along was she?” Annie asks.

“Four months.”

Annie quiets and starts sucking her lips in on one side.

She doesn’t hate Dad. Does that make me a worse person than her?

I don’t know how I feel about the pregnancy not taking. I want to feel sad for Lila. I know that I probably *should*, but I’m stopped by the lightness in my belly and a selfish whisper: *Maybe Dad will come back now.*

ocean jasper

I stroll across the school courtyard to Ernie and Bert, who are lounging against an old brick wall with their arms crossed, checking out all the girls.

Dozens of people mill about, talking loudly and laughing at things on their phones. The sun provides a steady heat, with only light breezes whipping at the posters plastered on the school buildings. Most of the benches are occupied by groups of three or four, except for his.

Jace sits alone on the bench in the middle of the courtyard, elbows on his knees, staring at his shoes. He's wearing black from head to toe.

I arrow through a crowd gossiping about the upcoming dance, and I weave around a pair of skateboarders. Considering the last time I spoke to Jace, do I even have the right to walk over there and say hi? Maybe it's the guilt, but something pushes me closer.

Maybe Dad will come back now.

The moment he notices me, Jace straightens his shoulders and slips on his mask of nonchalance. The cold stare he gives me doesn't tame the tiredness in his eyes or the slight puffiness at their edges.

"I didn't even know you went to this school," I say, sliding onto the bench next to him.

He shrugs. "Well, I do."

I want to acknowledge his mourning somehow, but guilt holds my tongue captive. I am beginning to feel sorry that the pregnancy didn't take, but I still can't silence that other whisper: *We're better than you.*

I wish I hadn't sat. Sweat glazes my hands and the backs of my knees. I instinctively search the ground for a rock, a pebble, a stone. Close to Jace's heel, a colorful beach stone with spots at one end seems to wink at me. If it represented the moment, it would be ocean jasper, a stone known for helping people cope with change.

I lean forward to pick it up, but I misjudge the angle and hit my nose against Jace's knee.

He shuffles to the side as I swing up, gripping the stone. Almost immediately—and even though heat is rushing to my cheeks—my breathing steadies. The smooth stone massages and revitalizes my skin as the sediments absorb my stress. I can do this.

"You're weird," Jace says, staring at my fist.

"You mean Dad hasn't told you?"

Now I *feel* weird. I glance away, but when I look back, Jace is eying me carefully, from my sandals to my turquoise shorts and white *Music Rocks* T-shirt. He lingers on the shirt. "He said you have a few ticks."

I nod. "Only this, really. But I flip out if I—" I decide not to go into the rest. What's the point? It's not as though we have to be friends now that our families are somewhat connected. "It doesn't matter."

I want to walk away but Jace catches my gaze. "Why'd you come over?" he asks.

I shrug. *Because it sucks. Raw nerves and lemon juice.*

He shrugs and mutters, "Not that I care or anything, but Dad misses you."

I try to shake off his words as I slouch my way to Ernie and Bert. Ernie might be short, but he makes up for it by being loud and obnoxious. But hey, friends are friends. At least I have someone to eat lunch with. "You look like your balls are being stung by wetas," he says.

Bert, who's big and beefy and plays rugby like he needs to

declare the gospel and convert everyone, punches Ernie on the arm. "You talk about balls so much I'm beginning to think you're a fag."

"Fuck off."

"Yeah," Bert says, "I don't think I'm having you over for sleepovers anymore."

Ernie flips him off and scooches over enough that I can rest against the wall. I drop my shoulder bag between my feet. Their shit-talking is stupid, but I know they don't mean it. At least, I hope they don't. Some people at school are known for getting stupid with their fists, though, and I steer clear of their radar.

"So what's up your ass?" Ernie asks.

I pull out a sandwich from my bag. "Nothing."

Bert and Ernie share a look I'm not privy to, but their raised brows suggest they're secretly plotting a way to get a real answer out of me.

They can try as hard as they like, but I'm not talking about Dad or Jace to either of them.

They prod a few more times but eventually give up and change topics. "Are we going to the dance or what?" Ernie asks, winking at a girl who looks like Annie.

"No," I say. "What's the point?"

This earns me a whack on the back of the head. "But there'll be tits galore—"

"Yeah," I say, and add a firm, "No." Because it's not happening.

And it doesn't.

Bert and Ernie go to the dance alone.

granite

The next six months, Jace is everywhere.

We never talk but he's always around; he's in the courtyard, in the music room, on the soccer field, or waiting for the bus on the other side of the street like he is right now. I'm waiting for bus 10 to take me back to Mum's; he's waiting for bus 02 to take him to Dad's.

A few others are hanging around. Annie is chatting to a large Maori dude, who's smiling as though he might get lucky.

I hang a few meters back and rest against the brick part of the school fence. On his side of the street, Jace has adopted a spot against a concrete wall with a book in his hand.

It's a pose we've been holding for months. We've perfected the art of pretending to read while surreptitiously peeking at each other. Looking without getting caught has become our game. When we do catch each other, we scowl and mutter various insults. I like "dickweed" best, but my exceptional lip-reading skills tell me Jace hasn't settled on a favorite insult, though he is particularly creative.

I open my geology textbook and stare blankly at a summary on plate tectonics. I flip a page and glance up. Jace is frowning into a brown book that's a shade or two lighter than his hair—still pretty dark. I risk staring for three counts before I fake-read some more.

I take my time and savor the tingling that prickles the back of my neck as Jace watches me. It's like a game of I Spy, but somehow it feels risky. Like we're two cowboys about to draw our guns. Like it's a contest to prove who is better.

I grit my teeth and mutter, "Dickweed."

A shadow falls over me, and I snap the book shut. The puff of air makes me cough. Jace has crossed the street and is standing in front of me.

"Little shit," he murmurs, but his lips are twitching at the edges as if he's holding back a grin.

"What do you want?"

"You didn't pick up a stone today." He gestures to the chipped brick at my feet. "You usually do."

"So you've noticed. That's a bit stalkerish of you, don't you think?"

He snorts and ignores the dig. "Dad's birthday is coming up."

I reign in the urge to shove him, opting instead for a tight smile. "Stop calling him your dad."

Jace shrugs it off. "He wants you and Annie there."

Dad's birthday is on Halloween, and his greatest wish is to make people love it. Halloween, that is. He decorates every year—well, he *used to* decorate every year. He'd invite all the neighbors to tour our haunted maze, then tally-up how many people screamed so he could beat his record the following year.

Our Halloween tradition was the best. We planned for months, practically the entire year. Jace and Lila won't even come close to pulling off such a feat.

This fact makes me smug, and my tight smile turns into a grin.

We're better than you.

Not at this.

"I'll be there," I say, hoping Annie will come along as well. Maybe Dad will tell us our Halloween birthdays are the best. He won't even have to say it because I'll be able to read his Frankenstein face.

"Really? You'll come?" Jace shifts, and the afternoon sun

hits my face.

I raise a hand to block it out. Jace corrects his position so I'm once again in his shadow. Even though other students are chatting, tires are bumping over the road, and somewhere in the distance an ambulance is calling, we stare each other down in silence.

"Okay. Cool." He turns, then swivels back. "Oh, and before I forget." He digs into his pocket and pulls out a small stone. He stuffs it into my hand. It's smooth and warm, like he's been holding it for a while. "Found it on my side of the road."

The sun pelts my face with bright warmth, and by the time I adjust to the light, Jace has crossed the road and taken up his spot at the wall.

We return to reading—or pretending to.

The duel has only just begun.

rhyolite

I hold the stone all the way home. It's a strange stone, this one. I have others of similar shape, size and sediment, but this one feels glassier and heavier as though it's laden with one-thousand-year-old secrets.

I whip out a magnifying glass and study the stone at our dining table.

It's an igneous rock, I think. Rhyolite, maybe? Could this stone have been born from the eruption of Mt. Taupo 27,000 years ago?

Maybe, but how did it end up on the side of the road at a bus stop of all places? Unless Jace picked it up somewhere else?

But why would he do that? Why lie about it if he did? Why am I still picturing his hopeful expression when I said I'd go to Dad's party?

I rub the stone until Mum asks me what's up. She knows I'm imbuing the stone with my memories, letting it soak up all the day's events, the highs and lows. I relax as the stone releases my tight knots and settles the fluttering in my belly.

Mum is hovering over the fruit bowl that's on the dining table. Annie isn't home yet. She got off the bus a few stops earlier with Mr. Thinks-He's-Getting-Lucky-But-Hopefully-He-Isn't.

"Are you still angry with Dad?" I ask quietly.

Mum leans back in her chair and sighs. "Yes. No, not really. I wish things could have been different, but they weren't. It might not seem fair to you, but for him and me, it is. We tried to make it work for you kids, but it wasn't working."

"He cheated on you. He made you look like a fool."

"Well, thanks for that." Mum hops off the chair and rounds the kitchen island to put on the tea kettle. She shakes her head. "I thought Dad talked to you about what happened. He didn't cheat."

"He had a whole other life, Mum! Five years with *them*."

"Lila and your father have been friends forever. But, yes, I suppose five years is when things broke down and couldn't be repaired." Steam curtains her expression, but her words are softly spoken. "Look, Cooper, we had an arrangement that we thought would work until you and Annie finished school, but like I said, it wasn't working. Your father was right to break it up. Right to go and live with the woman he's probably always loved. Right to let me have a chance to find someone of my own."

"Well that's . . . that's . . . *an arrangement?* That's fucked up."

"Cooper, watch your tongue!"

I laugh, squeezing my stone as if I might be able to juice it. "They're not better than us, Mum. They're not . . ." I wish Mum would rush over and wrap me into a hug, but hugs have always been Dad's thing.

Mum places a cup of tea before me. "Drink up, love," she says. "He misses you, and I think it's time you and Annie went to your dad's."

Relief overwhelms me. Someone else making the decision to see Dad for me? Perfect. Because the truth is I miss him too. So much. But I don't want anyone to think I'm taking his side over Mum's.

"I don't want to," I say pitifully. But it's a lie, meant only to comfort her.

And maybe my mum does know me the best, because she smiles and says, "You have to.

citrine

Halloween.

Mum drops me off. Annie is in the back seat, muttering under her breath. She's refusing to attend the party.

I open my visor to check my face paint—zombie face like always—and dip a finger into a thicker splotch of fake blood to draw it down as if it's dribbling from my mouth. The rest of my face is pale, except for my eyes, which Mum thought should be darkened with eyeliner. Disconcertingly, my eyes look brighter than normal, especially the one on the left. Then again, it's Halloween so I can get away with anything.

I angle the visor and look at my sister's reflection. She's staring toward the mansion much like I did the first time. She blinks and lifts a finger to dab her eyes.

I avert my gaze and snap the visor away.

My belly gurgles as I take in the haunted manor. Tens of jack-o'-lanterns with eyes like citrine gemstones line the path toward the flickering light at the front porch. I gulp.

It looks scarier than our house used to be. Scarier, better.

But their house is big—it has the advantage of looking creepy all on its lonesome. Inside will be the real test.

I crack open the car door. Faint, eerie music leaks from the manor and the moat glimmers as if being resurrected by it. *We're better than you.*

I hesitate. Do I really need to put myself through this?

The front door opens, and Frankenstein's monster steps out. Dad calls us over with a friendly, excited wave, one that hopes we'll race up and leave the past in the dust.

Wouldn't it be nice if life were that easy?

I smooth my ripped and dirtied shirt. It hangs out of my tattered jeans that are smeared with blood and ominous yellow ooze. "Pick me up in a couple of hours."

I drag my feet the way Dad taught me to zombie walk last year. I cock my head and let my tongue loll. I'm rewarded with a deep laugh. Maybe forcing myself out of the car was worth it.

"Stay away from me," Dad jokes, backing into the house. He shrugs and grabs me into a hug, whispering gruffly, "Thank you for coming. It's good to see you again."

My throat is tight. I swallow. "Happy birthday, Dad."

I don't have a gift for him this year. Does he notice? Does he care? Does he remember last year when I gave him opal cufflinks?

"Opals represent Zeus's celebratory tears after he defeated the Titans."

"Really?" he asked, putting them on despite being dressed for Halloween.

"It's also believed that the owner of this stone has the power of foresight."

He laughed. "See, it means I'm wise and you have to listen to me."

But would a wise man have fractured his family?

Despite that, I don't want him to let go. I want to stand on this cold porch with the light flickering above us for the rest of the night. Eventually, Dad pulls away. "Go on in. Take the tour. I'm going to scare this next lot."

Over my shoulder, a group of teens strut giggling up the path.

I duck inside. It's dark, the music's loud, and cobwebs hang over the windows. Signs written in blood direct the guests.

I follow the bloody signs to the staircase, where giant wetas hang from the ceiling with antennae that seem to be moving. Mum would have freaked out; she hates cockroaches and spiders, and the weta is both creatures combined.

A few people at the top of the stairs discuss which path they should take. They decide on slinking to the right, so I go left. I turn into the first room. Ghosts and werewolves and vampires hide in the shadows. Most are props but the vampire is real. He lies in an open casket, wedged into the corner of a room. His eyes spring open when a witch passes him and she jumps, knocking into a pile of fake chainsaws.

I catch one as it falls. It's made of rubber, but solid—

Something moves behind me. The hair at the back of my neck prickles. When I turn, though, it's gone. So is the vampire.

I shrug it off. I'm pretty sure this is an act to freak us out.

Isn't this whole thing ten times better than anything you and Annie ever did?

I drop the rubber chainsaw onto the table and leave the room. I wish I didn't have to wait for Mum to pick me up. I want to leave.

A door creaks behind me. A narrow slit of green light spills from a partially opened door. Someone whispers my name over the music. *Cooper. Cooper. Cooper.*

I slink toward it and pull on the handle—

I gasp. Inside the small closet, my name is glowing in the dark. Cooper. An illuminated arrow points to one corner. It takes me a moment to recognize the familiar shape—my old magnifying glass, laying on top of my journal.

I open the door wide and shuffle toward my name. It's hard to see in here. Coats are heaped in the corner and a shelf above my head forces me to squat.

Just as I grab for my journal, the door slams shut. I jerk around and feel for the handle.

My breath hitches and I start to feel dizzy. "Open, please, open."

I bang on the door, again and again. I need to get out of here—

I shut my eyes as the walls start to tilt and implode, ready to crush me. Instead of trying to escape, I fall onto my knees and frantically search the floor. If I can find a stone, the panic will ebb.

The walls will stop moving. I will be able to breathe.

I find nothing.

I sweep my hand over the carpet until I hit the pile of coats. I graze something hard and grab it.

It moves, and a slow chuckle follows. Coats shift and drop to the floor. Jace. I can tell it's him by his laugh. "Gotcha," he says.

"You dickweed. Get me out of here," I say through clenched teeth.

Jace laughs again and fiddles around with one of the coats. *Click.* A small beam of orange light flickers on and highlights the smug look on Jace's face. His fake vampire teeth glow.

I snatch the pen torch out of his hand and use it to light the door. "How do we get out of here?" The panic is detectable in my voice but I don't care.

"Can't."

I swing the torch back on Jace. He blinks and takes out his fake teeth.

"What do you mean you can't?"

"Can't open it from this side."

My breathing quickens again. "Get me out of here, Jace."

He frowns and leans forward. "Jesus, Cooper. Are you flipping out or something?"

I can barely nod. I rub my sweaty hands together and blink hard to restore my vision, which seems to be playing tricks on me. Is Jace coming closer? Closer? Bringing the walls with him? I slam my eyes shut and press my hands against my forehead. *It's going to be fine. This is all in your head.*

I hate Jace. I hate him for doing this to me.

"Th—this is payback for the soc—soccer ball thing?" I concentrate on my anger instead of panicking.

He rests his hand firmly on my shoulder. "Cooper?" Jace's breath hits my face but surprisingly it doesn't bother me. The smirk is gone from his voice and is replaced with concern. "Cooper, it's only a closet. I told my mate Darren to let us out in ten minutes."

"Wh—why?"

Jace shifts on his knees and leans closer. His hand lifts from my shoulder and wraps around my back. "Just concentrate on my voice, okay?"

"That's the la—last thing I want to h—hear."

He rubs my back. "Joking already. Knew it would work."

The truth is, the calm tone of his voice is soothing me. One point for Jace.

"It was meant to give you a little scare," he says softly, "not a huge one."

"Come on. You—you're going to piss yourself laughing about this later."

Jace freezes, his body tight at my side. "You don't think much of me, do you?"

"Wh—what else am I supposed to think if you shut me up in a closet?"

He doesn't respond with words, but he rubs circles on my back like I might start purring and fall asleep. "I've wanted to return your journal for months. I've been waiting for you to ask for it."

I shrug. "It's not a big deal."

"I read it."

"I thought so," I say. "I'd have done the same."

"So you want to be a geologist, huh?"

"Surprised?"

"Not really." He chuckles. "It's cool that you know what you want to be."

It's quiet for a long time, until Jace asks, "Do you really feel like you have to choose a side? Can't you be happy for both of them?"

A whoosh of air pushes Jace's question away, and I scramble out of the closet. Darren grins at me. After a few deep breaths, my sight clears and I recognize him as the big Maori fella who thinks he's getting lucky with my sister. *He better not!*

"You treat Annie with respect!" I say to him. I swing to Jace, who cannot look at me for long. I want to say something about him treating me right, but the memory of blood running down his nose stops me. “I guess we’re even.”

feldspar crystal

Annie slumps through the door and asks Dad where her room is. She doesn't look at him, nor come back when he returns from escorting her to safety. Today begins our first week with Dad, the Sunday after Dad's Halloween birthday.

Piano music loops and titters and darkens like grey clouds charging in for a summer storm.

I leave my bag in the entrance and follow Dad through the arched doorway into the dining room, where the table is set with jams and maple syrup and a stack of thin, flat waffles that resemble the pancake rocks in South Island.

"Your favorite," he says, rubbing his hands like he did when I was a kid. I'm not about to yell *Yippee* and lunge for the first waffle, but his effort lightens the heaviness in my belly. I sit across from him and glance toward the patio doors. Outside, darkness swirls like a brewing storm. "Lila will be down any moment."

I nod and stuff my hand into my pocket, where I'm stashing a feldspar crystal Mum gifted me this morning. Could she foresee my future? Why didn't she give me this crystal sooner?

I rub the stone and stare at the doorway to the side of the kitchen, waiting for Lila to appear. Lila, the love of my dad's life. Lila, the one who tore my family apart.

For a second I think of ducking under the table and hiding, but I can't avoid her forever. Instead, I count the plates. It looks like Lila won't be the only one joining us—

Dickweed.

He waltzes into the room with swagger, grinning at my Dad. When he sees me, his step falters but he quickly regains control. A hurried nod before he focuses on the table. The plates, the jam, the waffles, the vase of roses, the doilies.

He's going to play the game like this? Avoid me? Pretend nothing happened at Halloween?

"Looks de-lish," Jace says, skimming over me to Dad. "But I'm not hungry, so can I—"

Dad narrows his eyes into the familiar *stay right where you are* look.

The wind crumples Jace's sails; he sags into his seat and picks at the cushion.

"I want this to be a civilized morning," Dad says, pouring a carafe of orange juice. He continues quietly. "Be good to Lila, please."

As if his words started a countdown, Lila barges through the door not ten seconds later.

Spooky. Not as broad in the shoulders and not as tall, but the dark brown hair is his, and the blue eyes, and the straight nose that points up slightly at the end. She looks like she could be Jace's twin.

She smiles Jace's smile.

"Cooper," she says. "I'm so glad you're here." She kisses my cheek and ruffles my hair. She smells like potpourri.

Dad winces and holds his breath. I don't want to say anything nice or pretend I'm happy with this situation, but Jace is watching me, and even after what he did to me on Halloween, I can't simply grunt and play a moody thirteen year old.

"Yeah," I say, clearing my throat. "Thanks for the waffles. They're my fave."

Dad passes me the pancake rocks replica, a proud smile on his face. For that look, my choice to swallow my anger was worth the sacrifice.

The rest of breakfast involves Lila firing questions at me

and dad sharing embarrassing stories. Jace listens quietly, frowning at me every few seconds. When we're all finished eating, Lila begins cleaning up with Jace. Again, I'm stunned at their resemblance.

Dad clicks his fingers in front of my eyes and I focus on what he's saying. "Shall I show you your room?"

He leads me up a white-banister staircase that splits off in two directions. We take the left turn. "Lila and I are at the other end of the house," he says. "You kids have a bathroom down at this end, and a balcony." He slows as we pass the first room. A shadow falls over his face. "That's Annie's room," he whispers.

We pass a bathroom opposite my sister's room and a gaming room with a couch, bean bags, a stereo, a massive television, a piano, brass instruments, and music stands. A smaller version of the dining table fills up the corner of the room overlooking the backyard. Dad gestures to it. "That's where Jace practices piano and does his homework, but you have a desk in your room if you prefer."

"It looks completely different than two nights ago." I look down the hall to the next door. "Let me guess, the broom closet." I knock, but it's not a guess. I know. I also know it doesn't have a handle from the inside.

I hurry past it. Three doors are on my left but one of them is the balcony door. The other two face each other, with a few feet of cream carpet separating them.

"Yours and Jace's rooms."

Of course.

Dad braces the handle on the door to the left. "This is your space, Cooper. You can decorate it however you like." He pauses, glancing toward Annie's room. "You're always welcome here. I hope you will consider this your home, too."

I draw in a breath when he opens the door.

A double bed fit with a dark blue bedspread faces me. A desk rests by the windows, and a set of drawers with a mirror is perched on top of it. The walls are covered in square cubbyholes a couple of inches deep. They are empty, but for seven.

I recognize the stones inside them. They're the ones I left behind when I ran away the first time.

"Th—thanks, Dad."

He clasps my shoulder. "There's a port for your iPod by the bed."

I want to hug him. I want to turn around and *squee* like I'm small again, but I give him a nod instead.

"Right," he says. "I'll let you get settled in." He leaves, but it's slow, like he's reluctant to turn away in case I shut myself in my room like Annie does.

"I'll come down soon," I say, but my volume drops as I spot Jace shuffling down the hall. He doesn't see me. Ha! One point for me. He glances at the broom closet and bows his head the rest of the way to his room. I lean against the doorjamb.

He sighs, opens his door, and faces me. I open my mouth to say something, but I don't know what to say.

He rests against his doorframe and folds his arms. "It was a dickweed thing to do." He lifts his gaze to mine. "I'm sorry."

"I said we're even."

I close the door and collapse onto my bed. A brilliant flash of orange lightning flashes across the ceiling, reminding me of citrine and Halloween. The first sounds of thunder crack the sky. Shivering, I worm underneath my covers and wonder when the storm will end.

On my third week living at Dad's, I return from school early.

Usually I hang out with Ernie and Bert at Schmoos Café or the waterfront—anything to avoid the awkwardness of going back to Dad's—but I have a test for science tomorrow and I want a perfect score. I pull out the key Dad gave me and enter his castle.

Piano music sounds from upstairs; I'm heading there anyway so I move toward it. It's full and loud with tinkling interruptions. It's complicated, as if proving a point. The music stops and starts. At the fiddly-sounding part, a curse replaces the chord, and someone bashes the keys in annoyance.

I jog upstairs and stand outside the gaming room where the music is coming from. The door is ajar. I peep through the crack and stare at Jace, who's bent over the piano and knocking his head against the keys. I allow myself to watch.

Jace straightens, glances at his sheet music, and plays the piece again. Every now and then, his hands stray into my field of vision as he works the higher notes. His nimble fingers make quick, precise work of the notes and he easily dominates the tricky part.

It'd be too easy to slink off and pretend I didn't hear, so I push open the door and clap loudly, whistle even louder. Whether I like Jace or not, I appreciate his skills.

Jace practically flies off his piano stool. "Wh—what? You're home early."

"Test to study for." I drop my bag against the door. "You sound good."

Jace glances over his shoulder at the piano and the sheet music that fell as he leaped up.

"You like the piano?"

He shifts from foot to foot. "Yeah. So what?"

Why is he so defensive? "I meant it's cool. I like music."

He studies me, then sits back on the piano stool. "Yeah. I want to study music but Mum says the music business doesn't offer many jobs. Especially for a pianist." He shrugs. "But as they say, even if you can't do, you can at least teach."

I grin. "Keep practicing. I'm in my room."

"Won't be too annoying?"

I shake my head. "I always listen to music when I work."

"I start and stop a lot. Especially with this bitch of a piece." His smile tells me he loves the challenge of wooing the music until he owns it.

Is that how I look when I hold my rocks?

"Later, Jace." I drag my bag to my room, followed closely by Jace's "later" and the tinkling of keys.

* * *

Later comes sooner than I predicted. That night, Jace charges into my room and drags me out of bed. "Shhh," he says, jamming a finger to his lips. When I ask what the heck is going on, he presses his warm finger to my mouth. "Just be quiet, would you? Put your shoes on."

The light of the full moon slithers into my room through a gap in the curtains. Jace is dressed in jeans and a long-sleeved T-shirt that's inside out.

I pull on a pair of pants over my boxers, shove my bare feet into my Puma shoes, and shrug on a light jacket. I'm too curious to put up a fight or demand to know details. I follow him downstairs and out the backdoor. He closes it quietly. Usually a sensor light comes on but apparently Jace has disengaged it.

When we head into the thick of trees, my pace begins to lag. Pines loom above me, basking in a silver glow as they stretch toward the sky. "Jace, where are we going?" *And why are we out here together?*

Twigs snap and leaves crunch as he continues walking. "It's been bugging me," he says.

A breeze on the cusp of summer blows his words back to me. I quicken my step until I'm next to him. "What has?"

His lips part but he closes them and shrugs. I hate his shrug. I want to know what he's hiding.

"Come on." I shake my head. "You can't expect me to follow you out into the bush in the middle of the night!"

He smirks. "And yet here you are."

"Wipe the grin off your face." But I'm feeling one twitch at my lips too.

We walk around a bend of a hill where water from a creek tinkles nearby. At the bottom of a steep bank covered in tree roots, Jace stops. "I want to make up for shutting you in the closet."

I frown. Dragging me into the woods with a sinister smile is the way to do it?

He chuckles nervously and holds out his hand, which strikes me as strange. "Do you trust me?"

I shake my head. "Not really." But I grab his hand, which is rougher and warmer than mine. He leads me to a parting in the bank. "A cave?"

He squeezes my hand. "I discovered it last year. It's small, a bit bigger than the two of us, but it's cool. Keep to whispers inside, okay?"

He ducks into the cave and pulls me in with him. He's standing incredibly close so I can't see much else. For a second, I fluster, panic rising like it did in the broom closet. Why did he take me here! Why? Why? Why?

Jace whispers, "Wait. No. Turn around. Look outside. You're not trapped."

I gradually relax as I take in the vines and the curve of the stream.

Jace releases my hand. "Since you want to be a geologist, I thought you'd get a dig out of this." He smirks and steps back, opening up the view.

Hundreds of green lights speckle in bunches over the entire cave. "Glowworms!"

"Shhh."

"Sorry," I whisper. My stomach spins as though I'm standing on a cliff with my toes dangling in thin air. A wonderfully daunting rush.

"It makes me think I'm looking at the stars," Jace says, standing close enough that our sleeves are touching.

"Yeah. Stars."

I try counting the beads but I give up after fifty-seven. I'd rather watch Jace. "Have you ever counted them all?"

"No. Think it might be impossible."

"Like Stonehenge. No one knows exactly how many stones exist."

"Really?"

"One guy tallied them once. He recounted to make sure and he came up with a new number. Every time he counted, he came up with a different number."

The coolness of the stagnant air sends creeps over me. I rub my hands together and peer at Jace over my fingertips.

Jace beckons me outside. "You know a lot about rocks and stones, don't you?"

"As much as you know about music."

He slows his steps, staring toward the creek. "What is the difference between a rock and a stone, anyway?"

I move to the creek and stand on a large flat boulder. "They have different feelings." Jace joins me, his weight shifting the rock underneath us like a seesaw. We move instinctively to balance. "To me, a rock is massive—something that portrays strength. Rocks are complicated clusters of minerals that have baked for a long time."

I jump off the boulder to the stones edging the creek. Jace

gracefully leaps off too. I pick up a small white stone that shines in the moonlight. “A stone is a fragment of a rock. Like a snapshot of a bigger picture.”

“Is that why you collect them? A stone for every memory?”

I hand him the stone, forcing myself to ignore the heat that rises in me when my sensitive fingertips brush over his soft palm. “If you collect enough stones and minerals and heap them together, does it become a rock?”

Jace rolls the stone and lifts it midair. “I don’t know. Is this a moonstone?

“No. River stone.”

“Oh.”

“You sound disappointed.”

He shrugs. “Nah. Moonstones are pretty cool, don’t you think?”

“They’ve been revered for thousands of years,” I say as we re-enter the path. “Hindus believe that moonbeams form stones that can reveal your future if you hold it in your mouth on a full moon.”

Other than a shared smile, we’re quiet until we approach the trees that fringe Jace’s backyard.

“I don’t know if that would be a blessing or a curse. Knowing your future, I mean.”

“True, I guess.” Pine needles brush against my cheek. “It’d frustrate me to know all my future mistakes but not be able to stop them from happening.” He laughs.

We don’t exchange words until climbing up the stairs to our rooms. Jace stops me at the top. “I want to say something else.” I raise an eyebrow. He looks fleetingly at me and whispers, “We’re not better than you. I wish you wouldn’t think that.”

I pause. “What? How do you know—”

“You’re defensive.” He shoves his hands into his pockets. “I can read it.” He hesitates, then glances back at me. “That’s what I used to think of you and Annie. Before Dad moved here, I always wondered why. I thought it was because you were better than me and Mum somehow. But it’s not like that.”

My belly thickens like stodgy old porridge. “I don’t want to talk about it.”

“I just—” Jace starts, and I shake my head.

“No.” I move past him and charge down the hall. He tries to catch up behind me but I shake my head vigorously and he backs off.

pegmatite

Dad and Lila pile out of the rental van, and Annie, Jace and I spill out of the back in desperate need of stretching our legs. One side of my leg still hurts from Annie pinching me sixty miles ago. *Too cramped*, she kept muttering. The other side of my leg tingles from the friction of Jace's shorts rubbing against my knee.

Our first "family" trip—a day at Rainbow's End theme park—is happening today, the end of summer, a week before my second year at Newtown High.

"Sunscreen, guys," Dad says, framed by a distant Rainbow's End sign.

Lila smiles and passes Annie the sunscreen. Annie fishes into her day pack and pulls out her own. Lila shrugs and lowers the bottle.

I take Lila's offer, snap open the lid, and squeeze some onto my palm. Coconut—somewhat refreshing against the harsh heat of the mid-morning sun.

Jace's guttural sounds snatch my attention. He is standing a few steps away, yawning, arms clasped and stretched overhead. His T-shirt rides up past his hips, the print of a grand piano and illegible writing.

Neither of us slept well crammed in the double bed at the hotel last night. I kept tossing and turning, and Jace tried pushing me out.

He finishes his stretch and we exchange scowls—our routine, but usually when we're racing out of our rooms to stuff our school bags so we're not late.

"All right," Lila says, slipping between her son and me, herding us toward the entrance of the park. "Let's have a day of adrenalin and adventure!"

Annie slumps along behind us with Dad, who's telling her how much she used to love coming here. "Do you remember?"

"Yeah," Annie says loudly. "We went with Mum."

It's awkwardly quiet after that. We stand in line for ten minutes before Lila hands us our unlimited day passes. "Okay, so," she begins, but Jace and Annie skip off in two different directions.

I slip on my pass over my wrist. "Meet back here at four?"

Lila smiles. "We thought for lunch . . . never mind. You've all got money, I suppose." She shrugs. "Whatever."

Dad kisses her, my cue to leave. I thread through the crowd in Jace's direction. I'm not searching for him *per se*, but increasing my chances of running into him.

What for? I'm not sure. At Dad's house before the holidays, we were studying across from each other in the gaming room. He frowned at his papers and dropped his pen. "Why does brass discolor in air?"

I answered without looking up from my books. "Hydrogen sulphide."

After scribbling with his pen he whispered, "Thanks."

"Also, you know brass is an alloy of copper and zinc, right?"

Jace shook his head, and his lips quirked into a smile . . .

Screams from the roller coaster hit my ears, yanking me back to the reality of fresh popcorn and candied nuts, people lining up for rides, spilled Coke and discarded gum on the sticky ground—

Jace. There he is. Sitting at an octagonal table, straddling the bench, sunglasses perched on his head, texting on his phone. Lila allowed us to take them in case we needed something. Mine is vibrating in my pocket. Wait, vibrating?

A text.

I glance over the heads of a group of girls heading toward

the roller coaster.

I open the text. *Bumper cars have no line.*

A vague invitation? I accept. I'm not surprised the bumper cars have no line, considering they're not exactly the most adrenalin-pumping ride here. Jace startles when I straddle the bench in front of him.

I jerk my head toward the bumper car arena across from the cafeteria. "Let's go. I'll totally bump your ass." I meant *kick your ass* but it came out decidedly wrong and . . . weird.

I laugh.

Jace blinks rapidly and draws his sunglasses down over his eyes. "We'll see who bumps who."

Three minutes later, we're climbing into bumper cars and swiveling around on the smooth surface. Jace rocks to one end, me the other. He's taken his sunglasses off and his engine is *brrrr*ing. Other cars zoom around, bumping everything in sight. I narrow my gaze onto Jace and his car.

We move too slowly—it almost feels comical—but then we collide with a *thunk* and bounce off each other. Let the battles begin.

I slam into Jace repeatedly, and his car jerks back and slides. He doesn't laugh, but his eyes spark every time we hit.

I bump him into the wall he started from, and then I ram him into his corner right before the cars stop for the round.

We climb out of our cars laughing uncontrollably. "Told you I'd totally bump—"

"Never again!" Jace shakes his head but he's grinning. We exit the canopied ride and blink in the sun. Jace slips on his sunglasses like a Calvin Klein model.

We stop in the middle of the path. I feel awkward shifting from foot to foot in silence. What now? Do we part ways with a shrug?

Maybe I should leave before he does. That way, I'm in control. "Right. See you around."

Jace grabs me by the arm. "You're not going anywhere until I find a way to punish you for stealing my sleep!"

"So that's what this was?"

"What else would it be?"

He smirks and jerks a thumb toward the giant swinging ship. "How do you feel about rocky seas?"

"Not great."

"Perfect. We're going up there."

peridotite

I went to Mum's this morning for my fourteenth birthday but I'm at Dad's for the evening. We order fish and chips at the wharf, then stuff our individually-wrapped scoops of chips under our pullovers to warm us. We pull out chips from under our collars and pop them into our mouths. They're warm and deliciously salty-hot.

We head for the beach, where I crumple into the soft sand. Even Annie is with us, though she avoids Lila to sit at my side. Jace is perched on the stone wall behind us with Dad.

"We have gifts," Lila says. She rests a basket in front of my feet.

I unwrap two game-store vouchers, plus a new top-of-the-line magnifying glass from Dad. I thank them and pull out the last gift, wrapped as if someone fought with the wrapping paper and tape. "Yours, Jace?"

He groans. Sand squeaks under his feet as he crouches behind me. "I had no idea what to get you. It sucks."

It's a mug engraved with *I'm a Rock Whisperer*.

"I thought . . . you drink a lot of tea . . ."

I grin at him over my shoulder. "Cheers, Jace." He shrugs, and I say it again, quietly. "Thanks."

* * *

Nine months later, middle of summer, I'm scowling at my plate.

Capsicum. I hate it. Something about the tangy-burnt taste makes me want to retch. Unfortunately, the last time I didn't eat my capsicum, Dad served it to me for breakfast and every meal thereafter until I ate it.

I poke at my stir-fry, shoving the long strips of capsicum to the side of the plate. At times like these I wish I had a dog.

Dad and Lila are lost in a boring discussion, and Annie has inhaled her food so she can excuse herself. I scowl at her as she leaves the table, racing toward the capsicum-free zone of her bedroom to talk on the phone all night.

Jace has almost finished his dinner. Judging by his expression, he doesn't hate the dinner but he doesn't love it either. He shovels a few more vegetable bits onto his fork and glances over at me. Specifically, at the mountain of capsicum collecting on the side of my plate.

He shakes his head and mouths "breakfast," to which I groan and reluctantly stab one of the strips of disgustingness. Jace chuckles, glances at his mum and my dad still talking, and quickly pinches my plate from under my nose. In one swift scoop, he piles my capsicum onto his plate and slides my dinner back to me.

He shrugs, but it feels more like a wink. My smile is forged from somewhere deep as I tackle the rest of my food—

"Where's Annie?" Dad asks me. I jump, afraid we've been caught.

"Oh, Annie? She excused herself. You half nodded at her."

His mouth sets in a thin line as he takes in her empty place. Lila rests her hand next to his, their pinkies touching.

"No matter," she says. "We'll tell the boys first—"

"Annie!" Dad yells, pushing back from the chair. "Come back down here." He moves toward the stairs.

A few moments later Annie stomps back into the kitchen, sighing loudly. She hovers in the arched doorway, staring toward the patio instead of us. "What?"

Lila smiles brightly. “For our second family trip, we’ve decided to trek across part of Abel Tasman National Park.”

* * *

Another year rolls by. Annie and I combine our money to buy Jace a ticket to the Symphony Orchestra to see a famous pianist. A Christmas gift; the first Christmas we've spent at Dad's.

He accepts the ticket with a frown. "Thanks," he says. It's a soft thanks that follows me all day.

I get every gift I hoped for, including a new phone, a *To the Center of the Earth* board game, and a documentary on fossils. "Let's check it out!"

But Dad and Lila bow out, making up a quick excuse about getting up early.

Annie and Jace look at each other, excuses dancing unspoken between them.

"You don't have to," I say, shrugging and heading up the stairs. "I'll watch it on my own."

Annie races up the stairs and flings her arm around my neck. Her tightly-curled hair bumps on my chin. "Okay. I'll watch it."

I roll my eyes. She's playing nice, and I don't want that. "Nah, I'm good. Actually, now I think about it, I'm kinda tired. I'm going to bed."

"You sure?"

I drop her off at her room. "Of course. We can watch it this weekend." By then she'll forget about it anyway.

"Okay," she says and ruffles my hair. "Promise."

Her door shuts with a puff of wind, and I slink toward my room.

At my bedroom door, my foot brushes against something hard. Six stones are placed in the doorway at equal distances. I slip the documentary DVD under my arm to crouch down and pick up the stones. Limestone. Quartz. Granite. Amethyst. Aquamarine. And—I laugh out loud as Jace's padded steps clunk down the hall—a moonstone.

"Did you put these here?"

Jace stops a few feet away and leans against the wall. "Nope." Out of the corner of my eye, though, I detect a grin.

"They're beautiful."

He shoves his hands into his pockets. "Are they?"

"I love how they're squared. But if you didn't put them here, who did?"

"Someone who wanted to wish you a Merry Christmas." Jace meanders closer, then pulls the documentary out from under my arm. "I mean, I'm not tired. I was gonna watch TV anyway. Why not this?"

He ducks into the gaming room.

I pocket the stones and follow him.

part two: sedimentary

sedimentary: matter that settles

sandstone

With pursed lips, Lila throws a wet, moldy-smelling load back into the washing machine. She's pissed, but I can tell she's trying to hold it in. Like me, she hasn't figured out her boundaries or how far she can push into the parental role. The clothes make a loud slapping sound as she throws them into the barrel.

I stand with my thumbs in my pockets trying to cough up an apology, but it won't come. It really was a mistake. Completely unintentional. Besides, Lila always asks me to do work, never Annie. My sister hates her but I don't, so I get all the menial tasks? That sucks.

"I need you to be more proactive around the house," she says. "Use your initiative for once. Look around, see what needs doing and do it. Don't wait to be asked all the time."

She has a point, which makes it worse. I want her to be wrong so I don't have to swallow the urge to tell her to shut up. *She can't tell me what to do. She's not my mother!*

I'm shaking and my teeth are clenched. I'm about to yank the clothes from her grasp and tell her to have a break, have a fucking Kit Kat, when Jace strolls in.

He steals up to his mum and says, "Good afternoon, beautiful." He follows up his deviously-timed congeniality with a kiss on her cheek.

Lila's cool stare has melted. Before she can speak, Jace picks up the last of the clothes and throws them in the machine. "Darn," he says, "I meant to hang these out this morning."

Lila says, "No, that was Cooper's job."

Jace laughs this off. "Yeah, except he bet a week's worth of chores that he'd score higher than I did last year on the end-of-year exams." This is a lie—not the beating him part—that's true—but the betting part. We never made such an agreement. I want to catch his eye and ask what he's doing, but he refuses to look my way.

"You can't bet your chores away, Jace," Lila says, and her tone is soft now. Maybe she sees this falsified bet as us bonding. In any case, she sighs and claps Jace lightly around the head. "Next time tell me so I don't go picking on Cooper."

Lila gives me an apologetic smile. Then she says, "Since you're taking over Cooper's chores for the week, you can start chopping the vegetables for dinner."

Jace groans. I hope for his sake no onions are required. I've seen him cutting onions, and the colorful language that escapes his mouth as he dices is not pretty. He hates onions. He claims he can smell them for days afterward, and that it makes the piano keys stink when he practices.

When Lila leaves I slink up to Jace. He is concentrating on pouring in the washing powder but he twitches when I stand next to him.

"You didn't have to do that," I say softly.

"Yeah, I did," He shuts the lid of the washing machine. "You were about to get really mad at my mum. She already has a hard enough time with Annie." He starts the machine and turns around.

He was doing this for her, not me? I back away, hitting my hip against the sink. I'm embarrassed about how I acted toward Lila.

Jace rests against the machine and stares at me. Heat races to my cheeks, and I stammer, wishing to God I'd hung the stupid clothes out to dry this morning. "Sorry," I mumble as I spin for the door.

In two steps, Jace has my arm. "Don't get like that."

"Like what?"

"Like you'll avoid me for the rest of the week now."

I'd like to lick my wounds in private, thank you. "Avoid you? Hardly possible."

"You won't hole yourself away in your room the whole evening?"

Yes, yes, I'd like to do that very much. "Of course not."

Dammit.

Jace's grip loosens, and his fingers slip off me one by one. "Good. Because if I'm doing your chores all week, I want you at my beck and call."

"Your beck and call?"

Mischief lights his blue eyes. He may as well start rubbing his hands together the way he's looking at me. I can hear the maniacal laughter. "Yeah. I might have a few chores of my own that need doing."

I shake my head but I'm grinning. How can he have this effect on me? "You're going to milk this, aren't you?"

"Like a cow."

"Jace," Lila calls from the kitchen. "Start with the onions."

* * *

The entire meal, Jace stares at me with an evil, I'm-going-to-punish-you stare.

Dad taps his fork against his wine glass. "Listen up, kids."

I elbow Annie in the side when she mutters something about not being a kid anymore. After what Jace told me about his mum, enough is enough. It's time Annie accepts our new life.

"Lila and I have thought this over," Dad continues, smiling warmly at Lila. His eyes dance with joy. "This weekend we're taking our third family trip."

Annie's chair squeaks, but other than that she says nothing.

"What? Where?" I ask. I kind of hope we might go hiking again like we did last year. Abel Tasman rocked. I smother a chuckle at my wit.

"We decided on something outdoorsy—"

"White-water rafting!" Lila bursts out.

Dad squeezes her hand. "It's a two-day trip. Our gear will be transported to our camping site for us. So we'll be tenting."

"Tenting?" Annie asks. "Like, all together?"

"Well, no," Dad says. "We have two double tents and a single. We thought the boys could share a tent, and you could have your own."

Lila says, "Unless you want to share with your dad. I'm happy to have the single one to myself." She tries to engage Annie with a smile.

Annie shrugs. "I'm good with the single."

It's quiet for a moment. I fork a piece of broccoli and pop it into my mouth. The onion-garlic taste makes me smirk. I glance toward Jace's hands curled around his knife and fork. He's glaring at Annie, and I know exactly what he's thinking.

"I think it sounds awesome," I say cheerily. I mean it, even though I'm cheering more boisterously than I normally would.

I excuse myself after we finish eating, but I don't make it up three stairs before Jace calls my name.

He dries his hands on the tea towel thrown over his shoulder. "Since I have to slave in the kitchen," he says, "you have to do the same in my room."

"Your room?"

"It's a bit of a mess. Clean it up, would you?" He flashes a wide, mocking smile before returning to the kitchen.

For a second I contemplate ignoring his command, but I don't.

His room isn't bad. The bed is unmade and some clothes and shoes are lying around, but his desk is orderly. It's dark in here even though I switched the light on when I came in. His dark grey room features one turquoise wall. Cozy. I fight the desire to nestle into his blankets and curl up to sleep.

I get to work cleaning. With every breath, I inhale more of Jace. It's a slightly-sweet citrus smell, like oranges. His bedclothes feel softer than mine, well worn. I bring the cover up to my chin and nuzzle against it—but I instantly realize how weird of me that is to do.

I stop nuzzling and start making the bed.

The white splotches on his sheets make me blush. I try not to think too much about what a sixteen-year-old boy does up here, but the more I force the thought from my mind, the more elaborate is the imagery.

Bed made, I stuff his clothes into the hamper and straighten his shoes. I yank out one of his Chucks that's wedged halfway under the bed, and a few magazines slide out with it.

I blink at the porn in front of me.

It's the standard stuff that Ernie and Bert like to laugh at and get kinky with. I want to laugh but it's not funny. It's almost—enraging. I don't understand why this discovery angers me so deeply. *Not true, Cooper. And you know it.*

My throat tightens; I shake my head and grit my teeth against that voice in my mind—

Jace clears his throat behind me. "I changed my mind," he says. "I don't want you to clean my room."

I can't pull away from the magazines. Big-breasted women in slutty bikinis wink at me like they know exactly what I want. Bitches don't have a clue!

And why is that?

Shut up!

Jace crouches next to me and pries a magazine I didn't even know I'd picked up from my hand. He frowns and shifts. "I mean, if you want to borrow one—"

"No! Fuck off."

I stand abruptly. I can't look at him. Can't look at his bed. Can't breathe his citrusy air anymore. I stumble out of his room, shove on a pair of shoes, and hurry outside. I need . . . I need . . . I need a *stone*.

But I'm too close to the house. Its lights are illuminated as though it's watching me. Judging me.

I can't stand it. I have to get away. I jog along the stream through the pines, toward the cave. The wind sluices over my recently cut hair and tunnels down the arms of my green Koru T-shirt—the one Dad bought me for Christmas. The one that Annie said brings out my eyes in a wicked cool way and had Jace staring extra hard at me.

A stupid tear hovers in the corner of my eye, but I swipe it away as I duck into the cave.

The glowworms are extremely bright, but their magic takes a while to settle over me. When it finally does, I feel like I'm standing on the edge of that cliff again, about to fall. Thrills zip up my middle, stirring my cock.

I raise my arms and stand on my tippy toes to imagine the rush of falling into the stars.

Every inch of my skin tickles with shivers just like the last time I came here when Jace was at the creek, singing . . .

I drop my arms and snap out of the memory. It doesn't matter anyway. He didn't even know I was listening.

I sit on the floor of the cave, pick up a smooth stone, and hug my knees, willing the glowworms to rearrange themselves into an answer. An answer to my questions. *How do I stop feeling like this? How do I stop that voice in my head that lies to me and tries to confuse me all the time?*

The worms don't move. Neither do I. Not for a long time. I feel the heat of Jace's whisper before I hear it. "You're supposed to be at my beck and call."

I don't turn around. "What do you want?"

"Why are you hiding?"

"I'm not." I grip my stone harder.

He settles next to me, hugging his knees too. His arm bumps against mine, but I continue staring at the glowing green walls. "Why aren't we friends?" he asks. "Why do we pretend we don't like each other?"

"You give me a dirty look every morning. You tell me."

I hear him shrug. "I don't know. It's easier." He turns to look at me. His hot gaze on my cheek pulls me to face him, but I resist. "I know we were forced into each other's lives, but, I mean, I would have chosen you if I'd had the chance."

My breath hitches, and a shy smile stretches his lips.

"I mean, if I hadn't known you," he says, "and you stopped to talk to me that first time at school? I would've tried harder to hang out with you. I mean, you were odd." At this, he laughs softly. "I was surprised by the nose butt to my knee, but I liked you. And the *Music Rocks* T-shirt you wore is sort of funny now that I know you."

"I don't remember the T-shirt." The stone falls from my sweaty grip and I fumble for it again.

I would have chosen you.

My heart races as his words skate over every inch of my skin.

"What do you say, Cooper?"

I'm too fast to grab the hand he offers, and I hold it too tightly. I'm scared he can somehow hear that traitorous, whispering voice through my touch and he will quickly let me go. "Can we keep the dirty looks?" I ask.

He laughs. "With you, I think it'd be hard not to."

mudstone

White water rafting is terrifying. I'm being knocked around like a lollipop in a piñata, and for whatever goddamn reason, I'm hooting like I'm having the time of my life. The complexities of the mind: I will never understand it.

Our boat bounces over the rapids, swinging wildly. I clutch the paddle against my lap so I don't lose it again. At the front, Annie and Dad are laughing like wet hyenas, while Lila and our guide are enjoying an amused silence. Jace looks like he's going to be sick. Every time we're close to a rapid, his posture stiffens and his eyes shut like he wants it to end.

The boat dips abruptly, bashing me against Jace's side. I grab his lifejacket so he doesn't tip overboard. Another wave lurches into the boat, drenching Jace's swimming shorts.

"This is it," he mutters. "I see the news already. Seventeen-year-old boy drowns on the Waikato River."

"Sixteen. Birthday isn't for another month."

He pinches my thigh and I yelp. At least he's smiling now.

The rapids calm and we're back to paddling. Jace asks how much longer until the campsite, and Dad's answer elicits a groan. I chuckle at his whininess.

"Don't worry," I tell him with a cocky smirk. "You can hold my hand."

Annie and Lila laugh, which is the first time I've ever heard them laugh at the same time. Shockingly, they share an almost-friendly glance.

"This was a great idea," Dad says with a large inhale. "Fresh air and exercise. And look at the beauty."

Dad's right. The deep-turquoise water glows and its surface shimmers gold under the sun. A hint of a breeze protects us from overheating. Like Dad, I breathe in the smell of the river, the sunscreen, and all the good moods around us. Save Jace's, of course.

When the next rapid approaches, we pull in our paddles. Jace grabs the back of my hand and curls his fingers through mine, clutching tightly.

I stare at our hands on my thigh.

"You volunteered." Jace's grin instantly disappears as our raft bobs and twists.

This time, the Level 4 white-water waves exhilarate me, but the heat of Jace's palm and his sharp nails scratching into my skin excite me more.

The rapid lasts forever, yet it feels like the shortest bloody rapid there ever was.

When it ends and Jace pulls away, I tell myself I'm glad it's over.

But you liked it. You really liked it.

Leave me alone! Jace is practically my stepbrother.

It's not as though you're actually related.

He's also a boy.

Come on, I thought we were past this.

I'm quiet the rest of the day until we return to the campsite. After I help pitch the tents, I decide to bugger off on my own.

I find a cozy nook downstream that has its own riverbed, a small half-moon of pebbly shore. The stones hold the warmth of the day's heat, and I lie on them like a starfish to soak it up.

I empty my mind by thinking of nothing at all. I snatch up the first stone I find and drain all my negative thoughts and feelings into the stone.

Annie finds me an hour later. "What's up, bro?" She sits

next to me and gently peels my fist open. "That's pretty with the white layers," she says.

I sit up and look at it for the first time. Beautiful, smooth and curved like the nook we're sitting in or Cheshire Cat's mysterious smile. Did the secrets I poured into it make it appear that way? "Mudstone, I think. With a tiny quartz vein, see?"

"Looks too nice to be called mudstone."

"Mudstone comes in lots of colors and shapes. Makes up sixty-five percent of sedimentary rock."

"Hmm," Annie says. "Anyway, dinner's ready. I was sent to drag you back."

"What is it?"

"Couscous."

"What's up with you?" I lean an arm against her shoulder.

Her straggly wet hair presses against my skin as she rests her head on me. "I'm stubborn," she says quietly.

"You can say that again." I press my forehead against the top of her head to let her know I love her anyway.

"I don't know how to stop."

She starts to cry. Small wracking sobs that jerk her body.

"Hey, hey," I say, desperately trying to think of calming words. "It's not too late to make a change."

"B—but I can't. I'm a big bitch and I can't help it."

"You're not a *big* bitch."

Annie giggles, which soon turns into hysterical laughter. Her eyes are shut tightly, her nose squishes as laughter peels back her smiling lips, and tears stain her red cheeks.

I clutch my stone and Annie's laughter echoes in my hand. I know I'll feel it every time I touch the stone in the future.

Annie's laughter finally fades and she tilts her head at me. "I'm going to stop being a bitch. I don't want to screw up any more of my relationships."

"Any *more*?" I sense a story here.

She laughs again but it's a pained one. "Boyfriend dumped me. Said I was too passive-aggressive and bitchy. I wish I hadn't lost my virginity to him. Oh well. Better now than at university next year, I guess."

"Sorry. That sucks." This chat is quickly moving into awkward territory.

She doesn't seem to feel the weirdness because she keeps going. "Here's a tip for when you get a girlfriend: don't dump her two days after taking her flower. Don't take it in the first place."

I'm quiet. Too quiet, apparently. Annie sits up suddenly and I have to fight to maintain focus on my Cheshire stone.

"Cooper?"

I pick myself up. "I'll keep that in mind."

She doesn't take the bait. "Cooper—"

"Dinner's ready, right?"

She lifts a hand and I pull her up. She tightens her grip when I'm about to let go. "You know you can tell me anything, right? I'm here if you need advice or someone to talk to."

I force a grin. "Look at that. You're changing already." With an arm around her, I walk us back to the campsite.

* * *

After Dad's lame attempt at spooking us with ghost stories, we retire to our tents. At Dad's request, we pitched them with enough distance to quarantine Lila's snoring. This is a joke between them but out here in the bush it's taken seriously. I think Dad better watch his back.

In our corner of the campsite, Jace unzips our tent and holds the flap open for me. I bend over and drop to my knees inside the stuffy tent. Our sleeping bags are already unrolled so I set the torch to lamp mode and place it at the end of the tent, between our two sleeping mats.

Jace hooks his fingers under the hem of his T-shirt and peels it off. His chest is lightly tanned and tapers gently to his hips. He pulls at the few hairs he sports and grins at me. I jerk my attention to my bag and pull out a sleeping shirt. I'll wear the boxers that I changed into earlier.

"You got any noteworthy hair yet?" he asks.

Other than my crotch, I'm smooth. "Nah," I say and duck out of my shirt.

"It'll get there. Your voice has broken already."

"Is talking about puberty a fun conversation for you?"

He laughs and I shove on my sleeping shirt.

"We're friends, remember," he says. "We can talk about any shit we like." My back's to him but I know he's waggling his eyebrows. "The more uncomfortable, the better."

I have a feeling I'll need my stone tonight, so I take it out and climb into my sleeping bag.

Wriggling onto my side, I slide my hand with the stone under the pillow. Jace is yanking at the zipper on his sleeping bag. Finally it gives and he draws it up halfway and lays on his side, facing me in his threadbare blue T-shirt.

"You start then," I say. "With the uncomfortable shit. What about past or present girlfriends?" I hold my breath as soon as I've asked. Why do I care?

I don't.

Well, in a friend way I do.

"What makes you think I've had any?"

"Have you looked in the mirror lately?" I ask.

He blinks and it's hard to tell in the crappy lamplight but he might be blushing. I enjoy this thought until I realize the implication of my question.

"I mean—"

He chuckles. "Thanks, Cooper. You're going to knock the girls off their feet too, soon as you have a few hairs on that chest."

I rub the stone.

Jace rolls onto his back. Leaves from a low-hanging branch make the shadows on the tent's ceiling dance. The river babbles in the distance. "I met this one girl at Darren's last party—"

"What party?" I ask.

"Last weekend when you were at your mum's. Anyway, she likes me. She's a tall blonde with green eyes like—" I still. Like what? "Granny Smith apples," he says finally.

"That's—" Lovely? Great? Wonderful? Why don't they run

off and make some precious green-eyed babies already! "—that's precise."

He hums. "Yeah."

"What's her name?" I wonder if I sound too bitter.

"Susan."

"She's in your grade?"

He nods. "Not in my classes, though. Probably why I haven't noticed her."

"Is she as well-endowed as the pics in your magazines?" I definitely sound too bitter.

Jace faces me. "Why are you still upset about those magazines? Everyone jacks off to porn."

"I don't."

Jace frowns for a moment then nods. "I told you you're welcome to—"

"I don't want your crusty magazines."

He laughs. "I guess that is a bit gross. I can get you something fresh if you want. A few good online sites maybe?"

I want to knock my head against something hard. "No, it's . . ." *You really going to spill those beans here? While you're alone in a tent you have to share?* "Nothing. I'm good with the shower. Easy to clean."

"You're missing out. I have this lube—"

"Lube?" This comes out a yell and I slap a hand to cover my mouth.

Jace snorts. "You're fun. I can teach you so much. When you're fucking your fist with this lube, it feels so slick it has to be close to the real thing."

"Let's stop this conversation."

"You getting hard thinking about it? Me too."

I look down at the gentle rise of his sleeping bag—

"What about you?" he asks, tucking his hands behind his head. "Any girlfriends? Crushes?"

Saying no would feel like I'm admitting something so I nod instead. "Sure. Plenty." That should be enough to take the heat off.

And it does.

But I don't feel relieved. I feel like the biggest chickenshit ever.

* * *

When Jace finally drifts off, I crawl out of my sleeping bag, grab the light, and tiptoe to Annie's tent. I tug her foot and whisper until she stirs.

She gives a small jerk when she sees me, but quickly pulls it together.

We sneak to the edge of the river where cold stones sink under our feet. Moonlight reflects on the water, and the bush looks like it's painted navy-blue.

Annie shivers. I wish I'd brought us a blanket—

"Wait a sec," I rush back to the campsite, sneak back into my tent and slide out the sleeping bag.

"Here," I say to Annie, unzipping the bag. "We can huddle in this."

Our feet are still cold but our shoulders are covered comfortably.

"It feels different out here at night."

"Still. Quiet. Like a suspended breath."

"Nice."

She nudges her foot against mine. "Why are we out here, Cooper?"

"Have you ever felt so full of thoughts you think you could burst?"

She leans between her feet and picks up a stone. "When Mum first told me Dad was leaving us. All the anger, the questions, and that damn feeling of inferiority pounded in my head. I thought all you'd have to do was pull out a needle and prick, and I'd deflate until nothing was left. Sometimes I wished it too, so that I didn't have to feel sad anymore."

I wriggle my toes against the arch of her foot. "I feel like that right now," I say. "Angry, loads of questions, inferior. But also . . . butterflies. I'm totally excited but I hate that I'm excited. Hatred might be the biggest part of what I feel—"

"Cooper! Please, the suspense is killing me. Just—"

"I'm gay." I wait a second to let it sink in. "That's why there won't be any future girlfriends." Why I don't care for Jace's porn collection. Why I can't tell him all the uncomfortable shit.

Annie chuckles and says quietly, "That *is* exciting, Coop. You should let yourself be excited. Life has plenty of other problems to worry about, so don't let that be one of them."

This great advice is coming from my sister?

I hold my tongue and look to the tents in the distance. "How do you think Mum and Dad and everyone will take it?"

"I can't say for everyone but Mum and Dad will be fine. No need to angst over telling them. I know they won't care." She shrugs. "Might be a bit trickier at school though."

"Yeah, I don't plan on coming out at school. Just Mum and Dad. The rest can wait until university. Or until it's a need-to-know situation."

"Need to know? You mean if you find a guy you like? Is it too early to start matchmaking? Because Darren's cousin—"

"Too early!" I add a growl in case she tries to play Cupid anyway, and I hastily change subjects. "Whatever happened between you and Darren anyway? I thought he was your first."

Annie sighs. "I wasn't very nice to him a couple of years ago. I lead him on. When he asked me out I turned him down."

"Why'd you turn him down?"

She studies the stone in her hand then passes it to me. It's dark grey and long, like a dolphin. "He was too nice."

"How is that a problem?"

"Well, back then it was." She pulls the sleeping bag up to her neck. "I didn't want to hurt him, and I knew I would."

"But did you like him?"

She smiles. "Yeah. I still do. Haven't you noticed I'm always out of my room when Jace has him around?"

Until she said it, I hadn't.

I grin. "Why don't you apologize? Maybe you could try again."

"I sorta missed the boat on that one. He has a girlfriend now."

"Oh."

"But it's all right. Live and learn, right?"

"You sound like Mum."

The way Annie cuddles against me says she likes the compliment. We stay like this, sharing warmth and staring at the wide river and the inky tree shapes, until our eyelids droop and exhaustion sinks us toward the riverbed.

"I know what it is," I mumble through the last bit of consciousness I have left.

"What's that?"

"We all want to be a ten on the Mohs scale. But we're not. It's why I love diamonds." And the idea of not getting hurt.

She yawns. "Wouldn't that be nice?"

We use our last bit of energy to pull ourselves back to the campsite. Annie zombies off to her tent, and I drag myself to mine.

My sleeping bag is damp from the night air and the wet rocks. I shiver as I curl into a tight ball to keep warm. My teeth chatter uncontrollably.

I'm too tired to fumble around for more clothes. Jace stirs and I curse my shivers for waking him. His adorably sleepy voice says, "Huh? You cold?"

"I'll be fine," I murmur, except it comes out as a chattering of teeth.

Ziiiip. Jace lifts his sleeping bag. "Come in here. I'll keep you warm."

"S'okay."

"Don't make me drag you in here, Cooper."

Will he really drag me in there? I can't say it sounds terrible, but sleeping next to a pissed off Jace who can't sleep doesn't sound better. I pull my damp bag over to Jace. I slip one leg inside his opened bag and the warmth instantly cocoons my skin. I fold my body in all the way. His hot skin touches my arms and legs.

"Mmm. Better," he says, eyes drooping shut. "Better close the zipper or your back'll get cold." I twist to follow his instructions, but Jace quickly threads an arm over my side, finds the zipper and closes it.

My body refuses to ignore this intimate closeness with Jace's body. To stop a burgeoning erection, I shut my eyes and catalogue my favorite fifty stones, half of which have memories of Jace imbued into them.

I'm wide awake and warm again. Jace's eyes shut and his mouth hangs partly open. His chest rises and falls evenly, and I feel it against my own. I'm glad he's asleep so he doesn't notice my heart hammering against my ribs, my inability to breathe, or my shivering when his leg shifts between mine and pins me down.

My mind wanders to the magazines under his bed. I sigh, and sleepiness settles heavy and warm over me.

I'm hiding in a cave in the bush. I need to think. I hear Jace singing by the creek. Low and soft, his voice vibrates through the ground to my feet and into my body. I've never heard him sing before, but it's beautiful. I don't want him to stop. I sit on a tree stump and absorb the sad, sweet, familiar-sounding song that I've never heard before.

chalk

A week later, Annie and I go to Mum's after school. I wonder how long it'll be before I clutch the triangular chalk in my pocket like it's a lifeline.

"You're unusually quiet today," Annie remarks, opening the gate for us. "You all good?"

We shuffle up the path. "I'm fine."

"Sure about that?"

I nod. "No."

She loops an arm through mine and whispers, "Are you going to tell Mum?"

I resist grabbing my stone this soon. "Maybe."

"Want me to be with you?"

I shrug. "Yes. No. I don't know."

"I can wait in the study—just signal me if you want me to come out."

Annie's keys jingle as she unlocks the front door. "Hey Mum, we're home!"

Mum yells back. "In the kitchen!"

I kick off my shoes and beeline toward the scent of freshly-baked cookies.

The flour-covered kitchen is a mess of bowls, wooden spoons, and trays. Mum smiles and wipes her hands on her apple-print apron, which reminds me of Granny Smiths and that girl Jace likes. *Susan.*

I'm not hungry for cookies anymore.

Is it pointless to come out as gay when I don't even have a boyfriend? Maybe I should do this when I actually have someone to bring home.

This is your pathetic attempt at talking yourself out of telling her, chickenshit.

Annie steals a cookie off the cooling tray and juggles it until it's cool enough to bite. "These are good," she says with a mouthful.

"They should be," Mum says, ducking out of her apron and herding us to the dining table. She plants the cooling tray between us. "They're a bribe of sorts."

Annie and I exchange glances. What's going on here?

Mum paces, wringing her hands. Her eyes light up and she bites her bottom lip. Why is she so excited? Did she get promoted to a new job? Does she want to move?

My stomach lurches at the thought. I don't want to start over again. Besides, what would be the point of moving? It's Annie's last year before university and . . . Ernie and Bert and . . . Dad and . . . She wouldn't make us move now, would she? I swallow.

I grip Annie's hand under the table. She looks at me, startled. I guess she's not thinking what I am.

"What is it, Mum?" Annie asks, taking another cookie.

She nods and pulls out a chair. When she settles into it, she looks at each of us in turn. "I've met someone. We've been seeing each other for a few months now."

"Say what now?"

I couldn't have heard her right. Mum's here every afternoon when we come home from school. When—

We leave to Dad's for a week.

Oh.

Annie's cookie crumbles.

"His name is Paul. He's a librarian. I met him at Memorial Library in Lower Hutt, and well, we hit it off."

"A few months?" Annie repeats. "Why didn't you tell us?"

Mum takes a cookie but doesn't bite. "I didn't want to make more waves for you. I wanted to make sure it was serious before I told you about him."

"So it's serious then?" I'm trying to work through my initial shock. It's a weird thought that Mum has been dating some guy for months. Weird to know that someone else is creeping into her life—and by extension, our lives.

But I'm happy for her and I like her excitement. I especially like that she hasn't gotten a new job and we're not moving. I breathe out and smile broadly.

I squeeze Annie's hand. "Paul, eh?"

Mum nods. "Yeah, and he'd love to meet my beautiful children."

Annie sweeps up her broken cookie. I can tell it's taking her an effort to keep it together. She quietly excuses herself and throws the crumbs into the bin. When she comes back, she has a wobbly smile on her face.

"Do you love him?" she asks.

Mum hesitates. "I like him very much, and I definitely think I *could* love him. But to be sure, I need to know how he treats you guys. And what you guys think of him." She gestures toward the cookies. "Hence the bribe. He's coming tonight."

My words bypass my brain and spill from my heart. "If he makes you happy and doesn't care that you have a gay son, you have my blessing."

I surprise myself by scooping up a cookie rather than a stone. I bite into a warm pocket of semi-melted chocolate.

Annie shuffles her chair an inch closer to mine, while Mum puts down her cookie and walks around the table to my side. "Stand up, Cooper."

I swallow hard and pass my cookie to Annie. With shaky legs, I stand up and face Mum. I am an inch taller than her but she lifts herself onto her toes so we're even. She cups her hands on either side of my face and studies me. Her thumbs outline my brow and nose. "It's not a joke," I croak.

Her eyes well up and she kisses my cheek. "You're beautiful.

I love you. I support you. I'll always be your biggest fan, and I'll always cheer for you on the sidelines no matter what play you make."

She hugs me stiffly because Mum isn't really a hugger, but it makes me warm. "Thanks, Mum."

She rubs my arms and steps back. "Promise me you'll wear protective armor."

Annie snorts and I chuckle too—though mostly in embarrassment. But yeah, I'm well-versed in safety, thanks to Dad.

"When is Paul coming?" I ask, eager to change the subject.

Annie smiles and nods. "Yeah," she says. "When do we get to grill him?"

siltstone

Dad and I are cleaning up the dinner pots and pans. He washes, I dry.

"How would you feel if I brought home a girlfriend?"

He scrubs harder at the pot. "You're too young."

I'm almost sixteen. But I let that slide.

"What if I brought home a boyfriend?"

He pauses. "Still too young."

When we're done, Dad peels off the bright yellow gloves and says, "But when you're older, I'd sure like to meet whoever you bring home."

And that's it. We don't mention it again.

apatite

Jace is practicing the piano when I race upstairs. It's a complex bouncy-sounding song that perfectly matches my mood: complicated and exhilarated. I burst into the room and the door swings wildly, banging against the wall. Jace stops mid-song, fingers poised over the keys, head swinging toward me. His expression morphs from shocked to amused to cocky. "What's got you all excited?" His brow arches.

I feel good. So damn good. Like one-thousand pounds has been lifted off my shoulders. Part of me still feels anchored down but I'm ignoring that part for as long as I can.

"Keep playing," I tell him. Jace squares his head toward the music and begins again. I jump up and down, bouncing and dancing behind him like I've gone bonkers.

I don't care.

When I can't dance any more, I collapse on the couch and laugh. Even when Jace stops playing, I'm still laughing. And when he charges across the room and looms over me, I still don't stop.

He grins at me. "What the heck is going on with you?"

I press my foot against his chest to stop him from coming closer.

"You can't act this crazy and not tell me!" He clasps my foot and peels off my sock. "Tell me, or I tickle."

"It's nothing."

He tickles. I squirm to get free, laughing harder.

"Let's try that again, shall we? What's going on with you?"

"Absolutely nothing."

His tickle works its way up my calf to my knee. I buck, trying to kick him off. "Too ticklish!"

"Then tell me the truth." He wiggles his finger threateningly but I shake my head.

"Fine, but you asked for it."

Jace straddles me, his ass pressed against my lower stomach. He leans forward and tickles my armpits.

I scream out in laughter, and tears stream down my face. I lift my hips to buck him off but he takes it in stride, rising and falling with me. He shoves his cool hands under my T-shirt and my body arches with yearning. *Keep touching me like this! Yes, skate your fingertips over my chest. Keep tickling me like this forever.*

Jace stops moving and looks down at me solemnly. Our gazes clash. His dark blue eyes remind me of blue apatite, a mineral of inspiration, creativity, and awareness.

Awareness. I'm aware of the way he's sitting on me, aware of his warm weight and the pressure of his fingers against my chest. Aware of the blood that is making my cock hard. Aware of the electrical buzzes that pass through me as he continues to stare.

My breath hitches. Jace sits up, dragging his fingers off me. I can't be sure but I think they are shaking. "Tell me," he pleads.

I swallow, praying he doesn't shuffle back further or I won't need to tell him anything. I want him to stay where he is but I gesture for him to get off. I hurriedly fold myself into a less conspicuous position. "The thing is . . ."

Footsteps pound down the hall and throw me out of the moment. I try again. "Thing is—"

Annie flings open the door. "Jace." Her calm voice somehow turns me cold. "Your mum is crying. I heard them downstairs."

"She's back?" Jace rushes toward the door. "I thought she was working late." Jace hurries downstairs.

"Do you know why she's crying?" I ask.

Annie shakes her head. "Dad was comforting her. He looked upset too. I came right up here."

I bite my lip. Has Dad told her about me and she's crying for my soul? Will Dad change his mind about being okay with me?

Calm down. Lila has never been narrow-minded. This has nothing to do with you.

But what if it does?

We wait for Jace a while and slither off to our rooms when he doesn't return.

I place today's stone in a shelf above my dresser. I stare at it for a few minutes until I hear Jace behind me. He slumps through the open door and sits on my bed. I turn, lean against the dresser, and watch him. He's frowning and staring into the space between us.

"What's the matter with your mum?" I ask carefully.

He glances at me. "She won't tell me but something's up."

"I'm sorry."

He draws with his foot against the carpet. "It'll be fine, I'm sure."

"Yeah," I say, hoping to console him. "It'll be fine."

Nodding, he draws in a breath. He speaks but he's not really paying attention. "So what were you about to tell me?"

I shake my head. I can't tell him now, and I don't know that I would have before either. Coming out to him is not the same as it was the others. With Jace, it feels like I have more at stake—more between us that can break—and I'm not ready to deal with those consequences.

I know I have to do it eventually but . . . not yet.

flint

Over the weekend, Jace buys a used car, a small faded-teal hatchback that reminds me of mottled flint. But it works and it's rust-free. He takes me for a drive around the block, though technically this is illegal on a restricted license.

We stop at the beach, where I run in to the local dairy to buy us ice cream. We lick our ice creams while we stare at wisps of sand whipping across the beach. The choppy water is enjoyed only by a couple of surfers.

The sweet vanilla ice cream tastes good, but the silence between Jace and me feels bad. Since he found his mum crying, his mind has been elsewhere.

Jace slumps into the front seat and rests against the headrest, ice cream melting down his fingers.

"Nice buy," I say, patting the dashboard. "Think of the freedom you'll have now. No more buses."

He grunts.

Why'd you invite me to come along for the ride if you're not going to speak?

After we finish our ice creams, he gestures for my rubbish and disposes of it in the bin outside. He wipes his sticky hands on his jeans on his way back to the car, then stops. He bends down and picks something up. His back is mostly to me when he stands so I can't see what's in his hand. For a fraction of a second he looks at me, then he slips his find into his pocket and hops back in the car.

His pocket bulges a bit and I recognize the shape. A smile stretches my lips and it won't go away. I stare out the passenger window so Jace doesn't wonder why I'm grinning like a madman. When I regain my cool, I ask him what we're doing next since we have the whole day to kill.

He looks at me for a long time without speaking. I lean over and pinch him.

"Ow! What was that for?"

"You've been lost in your head for days. It's time to snap out of it."

He opens his mouth to protest but slams it shut again. He starts the car, throws an arm around the back of my seat, and backs out of the park. The heat of his arm at my neck makes me shiver, as does the confidence with which Jace drives. He likes it and he's good at it.

"You don't understand," he says around the corner from home.

"Then make me understand, or do something about it so you can get back to the real you."

Jace slaps a hand on my thigh and then pinches me back. "Stings, doesn't it?"

My mouth is dry. All I can do is nod because I still feel the weight and warmth of his hand clasping my thigh the moment before he pinched it. The shocks are still shooting to my groin and making me hard.

I shift, hoping my hardness isn't noticeable. Thank the stars he's concentrating on driving.

At home, Jace races up to his room and I wander about the house aimlessly like I'm living in the clouds. I don't know what to do with myself. I feel tingly and happy, like no one could piss me off even if they tried.

"Good, you're home," Dad says in the dining room. "I have a chore for you."

"What's that?"

Dad raises a brow and a chipper attitude. “The two upstairs bathrooms need cleaning.”

“Fun,” I say, rolling my eyes but following it up with a grin.

He observes Lila preparing lunch. “Where’s Jace?” he asks. “I have an extra fun chore for him.”

“Better than scrubbing toilets?”

Dad jingles his car keys. “Since he has his own car, I figure he’ll want to keep it clean. He’s going to wash mine while he’s at it.”

“He’s in his room.”

“Tell him to come down.”

I comply. Jace is on his laptop when I push his ajar door, and he hurriedly shuts it when I call his name.

His face contorts when I relay the menial task Dad gave him, but he gets up.

I start cleaning Lila and Dad’s bathroom. They have their own sinks, which is a real pain in the ass since I have to clean both.

Jace strolls in the moment I finish vacuuming. He’s wearing a raggedy T-shirt with a hole near the hem and a pair of soccer shorts. He moves over to Dad’s sink and plucks his toothbrush from the holder.

I unplug the vacuum cleaner. “What are you doing?”

He holds the toothbrush up. “Time he replaces it anyway, don’t you think?” He edges to the door where I’m standing. “This’ll make our tire rims shine.”

He jumps past me and strides down the hall, but he stops suddenly. “I almost forgot,” he says, coming back to me and digging his free hand into his pocket. “This is for you.”

He throws it to me. It’s a quartz pebble, peach with a vein of white running through the middle in the shape of a wave, and it’s still warm from Jace’s pocket.

I look up to thank him, to tell him it’s amazing.

But he’s gone.

rock salt

The night before Jace's seventeenth, he leaves to party at Darren's house. I'm not invited but I have an essay to finish anyway. Jace's birthday is tomorrow, and I don't want this stupid assignment hanging over me.

I sit at my desk to finish my essay. When the clock hands indicate twelve o'clock, I smile and text Jace happy birthday. Ten minutes later, I jump into the shower, jerk off, and ready myself for bed.

I'm climbing into fresh sheets when my phone rings. I fall out of the bed and knock my head against the carpet.

I rub my head and find the damn phone. Jace. But I knew it was him the moment the phone rang.

"Happy Birthday!"

He groans. "Happy? I don't know. What is happy, anyway?"

"Are you drunk, Jace?"

He burps and that says it all.

"Can you pick me up, Coop? I left my wallet at home and I'm too drunk to walk home."

Shit. "I only have my learner's permit." And no car—

Annie's car. She got picked up by a friend earlier so her car's available.

"Please? I don't want Mum or Dad to see me like this."

"I'm on my way."

I pull on a pair of jeans over my boxers but I leave my nightshirt on. I don't plan on socializing. After shoving on some shoes, I snatch Annie's car keys. Jace has taught me all the tricks to sneaking out without getting caught—I make sure to switch off the sensor light before leaving.

I climb into Annie's run-down Honda parked halfway down the street. I start the car and pray I don't get pulled over.

I'm in luck, and after a quick stop, I arrive at Darren's fifteen minutes later. The house is swarming with teenagers in various stages of sobriety and undress. I weave around giggling girls and couples making out, and follow the pounding beat of the music to the heart of the party—the drinking games.

And Jace.

A guy pushes past me, slopping beer out of his paper cup. I jump back so it doesn't hit me. Close.

Jace is sprawled face down on the couch, one arm touching the floor, his feet sticking over the end of the couch, and a pink streamer hanging over his calf. His T-shirt has risen up, and the hard plains of his back and the curve of his hip are on full display. He seems to be searching the crowd.

When he spots me, he transforms. His body sparks with life and he pulls himself off the couch. "Cooper," he mouths as he crashes toward me.

"Brother's here to pick you up, eh?" Darren says as he throws an arm around Jace's shoulder and walks the rest of the way with him.

"We're not even *step*brothers," I mutter, but this is mostly to myself—and the punk guy at the booze table next to me.

"I told him not to drink so fast," Darren says when they catch up to me. "But he was nervous." His thumb jerks to a bunch of girls in the corner of the room.

I immediately recognize the blonde, who has just slopped red wine down her front and is laughing about needing salt. Someone tells her to head for the boys drinking tequila.

I know she'll have to pass us to get to those boys. "Right," I say. "I'd better get him home."

Jace mumbles something but the slurring music pounding in my ears deafens me. I say good-bye to Darren and take his place, slipping an arm around Jace and steering him out of the party.

He's not so drunk that he can't fold himself into the car, thank God. But he jerks the seatbelt and it doesn't extend. I know it's a fiddly fucker to deal with when sober so I lean over and draw it out for him.

Jace's glazed eyes match his amused smile. "What?" I ask as I click him in.

He shrugs and rubs his temples. "I need some water."

"Glove compartment."

"You're a lifesaver."

He drinks while I drive us home.

When he stumbles out of the car, I notice his wallet bulging in his pocket. I shrug it off. He was probably too drunk to realize he had it all along.

I lock up the car and sneak us back into the house.

Upstairs, he goes to the bathroom. I figure he's good and climb back into bed. Two minutes later, my door opens and Jace flops onto the bed next to me.

I roll over to turn on the bedside lamp.

"Wrong room, Jace."

"Nope," he says, sounding a little less slurred now. "The right one." He's stripped down to his Angry Bird boxers and is lying on his belly, arms under his head, looking at me. "It's my birthday, and I want to chat."

I shuffle back against the headboard. "How was the party?"

"Okay, I guess. Not great."

"What did you do all evening?"

"Talked about bullshit. Drank. Started some games."

"Games?" I know what games he's talking about, so now my belly is lurching.

"Childish. They thought they were being so funny. Got put in the closet with Susan and I nearly puked all over her."

I'm relieved. "Suave."

"I didn't want to play anyway."

Ernie and Bert are always trying to get such a chance. "Why not? Thought you liked her?"

"I do but that's not the way to start a relationship. I want to take her on a few dates first. Flatter her. Spoil her. Let it progress from there."

I loathe every word. "She must be special then."

"I hope so." Jace shifts his attention to the shelves behind me. "The stones above your bed. Those are your favorites, aren't they?"

I glare at them and shrug. I want to kick him out of my bed. I want to slam the door and be alone. I want him to stay right where he is until he opens his damn eyes to what's in front of him. "My favorites from the weeks I'm here."

Jace pulls one out, the amethyst he denied giving me. "What's this one remind you of?"

"Do you like it?"

"It's my birthstone," he says. "I kind of have to like it."

Just as I thought. The stones he'd given me back then meant something.

"So what does it mean?" he asks. "What do you think about when you look at this one?"

"I think about you, actually," I say while refusing to look at him. "You probably don't remember but it happened last year. We were watching classics with Annie. When she went to bed, we stayed up and watched Silence of the Lambs, and it freaked the shit out of me."

"I remember," Jace says, and his voice tickles the hairs on my arms and makes my neck prickle. "You were trying to be all tough like you could handle it but your shudders were vibrating the couch."

"Hardly."

"Coop, I was about to turn it off and send you to bed."

This I didn't know. "Why didn't you?"

"Because you kept saying these stupid jokes," his voice changes pitch. If he's mimicking me, he's doing a poor job of it. "When does a cannibal leave the table? When everyone's eaten!"

Jace chuckles. "You kept asking if *I* could handle it. I knew you were determined to get through it. We each need to have a movie that freaks us the fuck out so we can laugh at ourselves later."

I growl at him and swat the back of his head.

"That's what the amethyst reminds me of," I say, though that's not all of it. I also remember when Jace grabbed a blanket and stopped himself from tossing it to me to lay it over both of us. We were sitting with our feet curled to the middle of the couch, the rest of our bodies as far from touching as possible.

Then I got a fright and my foot slipped against his. I waited for him to jerk away from me and rearrange himself, but he didn't, and for the rest of the movie our feet were touching.

Suddenly Jace clears his throat, puts the stone away and pulls down the white Cheshire stone, the most recently added favorite. "And what about this one?"

"That one's kind of personal."

Jace smirks. "Remind you of your first proper wank? Your first French kiss?"

"You're drunk."

"Yeah. But that gives me courage."

"Courage to do what?"

"To ask you."

"Ask me what?"

"Why don't you tell me?"

"Is this a trick question? Sounds pointless."

"You don't get it." He sighs and picks up another stone. "What about this?"

That one I can tell him.

After I finish the story, he smiles and yawns. "I want to see one more."

"What's that?"

He holds out a hand and rubs his fingers. "Today's stone."

"Today's?"

"That's what I said."

I slink out of bed and retrieve it from a cubbyhole above my desk. The stone is a layered slice of sediment I found at the local park down the road when I rehearsed my speech for Jace's birthday. I couldn't think of the right words so I picked up the stone in frustration.

I pass it to him and he eyes it carefully, as much as a drunk guy can. He sniffs it and touches it with the tip of his tongue.

It's fast becoming one of my favorite pieces. He hands it back to me and I set it on the side table.

Jace yawns again. "Can I sleep here, Cooper?"

"Why?"

He shrugs. "Warmer with you next to me. Be like camping again."

I shiver. I want to beg him to sleep in his own bed, to dream of Susan there, but I'm too weak because I want him here, so I can pretend he's mine.

"You can crash in here on one condition."

"What's that?"

"You have to get up early with me. I have something for you."

"How early are we talking?"

"Very. We need to head out while it's still dark."

"Okay."

"Okay?"

"Good night, Cooper."

"Night."

His hand fishes for mine and when he finds it he draws lightly over the back. "You're the best friend and brother I could ask for."

Friend.

Brother.

I especially don't like the second word. It's trying to snuff out that little flame of hope in my belly, and I don't want it to.

I switch off the lamp, drowning the room in shadows and secrets, and lie down.

Jace lulls me to sleep with his heavy breaths.

Sometime in the night, he cuddles under the blankets and drapes his arm around me. It's warm and solid there. Different, but it's a good different. I leave Jace right where he is and continue sleeping alongside him.

He groans when I wake him, and he curses when I make him follow me to the cave. It's later than I'd have liked. The sky is a milky grey but it's still dark enough that the cave glows with clusters of green light.

We're always quiet in here. It's the perfect place to give him his gift.

We sit down in the cave, cross-legged and facing each other. The darkness and glow give us a greenish aura. Jace shifts and his knees bump against mine. He's watching me, waiting for me to speak.

I breathe out and dig into my pocket for his gift, which is wrapped in a black velvet bag. I finger it through the soft bag, and its meaning weighs heavy in my hand. I've been looking forward to giving this to him for weeks but now my hands are clammy and my tongue seems to be stuck to the roof of my mouth.

I draw out the gift and, without speaking, lift his hand and press the gift into his warm palm. He stares at me, then stares at his hand. His Adam's apple juts out with a swallow.

"Cooper—"

I lift a finger to my mouth and shake my head. I want him to like it, to accept it, not to speak.

He trembles as he opens the bag and draws out the greenstone fishhook. It's simple and dark with flecks of lighter green. I hope when he looks at it he sees me looking back at him. I hope when he wears it, we—us and the times we've had together—will be in his thoughts.

I know seeing it against his chest will remind me of the moment we met, when I hated him. Hated him for claiming my dad as his own, hated him for giving me that cocky grin, and hated him for taking my breath away. Because it was that single moment when it all clicked. When my body screamed to me how attractive he was, but I twisted it into something dark and ugly. His blue eyes weren't beautiful, they weren't. They were the color of the rubbish bags Mum used in the bathroom; the color of oily seawater; the color of regurgitated fish scales.

I glance at the hook he's tying around his neck. It had to be a hook because I want to reel him in. Even if I can't or won't, it'll be nice to see hope hanging from his chest.

Jace stuffs the empty velvet bag into his pocket and stands up. I follow. Outside the cave, Jace turns to me. He doesn't hug me. In fact he keeps his distance. The creek babbles. Birds chirp. And then his words. His promise.

"I'll never take it off."

* * *

Lila and Dad take us to lunch to celebrate. We're at a restaurant on the waterfront and we're all dressed up. I've managed to spill water on my shirt and I'm mopping my chest with a napkin. Annie is laughing and shaking her head at me. Dad is content, resting back in his chair, looking out over the glittering sea at the view of the city.

Lila sits on the other side of her son, her eyes rimmed with moisture, squeezing Jace's hand. "Seventeen," she says. "I can't believe how fast you've grown up."

Jace kisses her cheek. "I still have a year at home before university."

One more year.

Only one.

Then he's off, and what about you? You're still going to be in school. Two different worlds. He'll keep in contact for a while, but it will fizzle, and eventually you'll merely be guys who grew up together, and the friend part will end.

Dad swivels toward Lila, a melancholic smile playing at his lips. "Do you remember when we were seventeen?"

Lila laughs and releases Jace's hand, scavenging for her glass of orange juice. She's about to drink when she stops. "I was sad most of that year," she says and Dad frowns, sitting up straight.

"You were?"

She sips her orange juice. "Yes. Hard not to be when your best friend goes to the States for six months."

"You had what's-her-name. I thought you were fine. You always raved about how you two were having all sorts of adventures. Made me jealous half the time."

Lila looks surprised. "It did? I guess that was the point. I was having a miserable time but I wanted you to miss me."

Dad turns in his chair so he's facing Lila directly. He takes her hand and kisses the palm. "You have no idea how much I missed you."

Annie clears her throat. "Maybe we should check the menus before the waiter gets here." I read her tightly spoken words. *What about Mum? If they were already in love, how did he ever fall for Mum?*

Did Dad ever love her? Certainly not truly, madly, deeply.

I stare at the three sets of knives and forks before me, polished to a shine.

Jace shifts and fiddles with the edge of the white tablecloth. A silent storm of emotion brews at our table. Lila and Dad are lost in the past, lost in each other. The rest of us are lost in various degrees of hurt.

Except I don't understand why Jace is hurt. He and his mum won, so shouldn't he be grinning?

Unless he feels bad for us.

I have to break the tension before Annie notices. She's been perfectly open and loving since our camping trip, and I don't want her to regress. "Is that where you were converted into a Halloween freak?"

Dad and Lila drop hands and Dad laughs. "You could say that."

The rest of lunch is pleasant, though stiff. Every now and then Jace touches the hook making a bump in his shirt, but he only looks at me once to laugh when an oyster pops free of its shell and lands in his water glass.

After dessert, his mum asks, "What's that you're hiding under your T-shirt?"

I freeze. I'm not sure why exactly. It's only a gift after all.

But it's intimate. They'll take one look and know.

Jace glances at me, reads my insecurity, and tells her he bought a necklace.

"You know you shouldn't buy your own greenstone," Lila says. "It's only meant to be given to you by someone who loves you."

"All this talking about stones," I say, trying to shake off the unexplainable shivers zipping up my spine. "You'd think it was my birthday."

Dad laughs. "Have you given Jace his stone yet?"

"Huh? No, he said he bought it himself!"

A small frown shadows Dad's face in confusion. "I mean his birthstone. All the rest of us have gotten ours. What is February anyway?"

I let out a relieved breath. "Amethyst. Which really would make the perfect gift. It's believed to sharpen wit, after all."

Jace laughs and elbows me in the side, scowling. The light nudge sends a whole other set of zings running through me.

"Also," I say, our gazes catching for a second, "it's thought of as a composer's stone."

Lila claps. "Yes. How perfect."

When we arrive home, Jace checks the mailbox instead of going straight inside. I wait for him on the porch. He's staring at a large brown envelope as he slowly dawdles up the path. He notices me watching him and hurries his step.

He rolls the envelope up and holds it at his side. "What're

you waiting for?"

"Want to play video games?" I gesture to the mail. "What's that?"

"Nothing. Just university preparation stuff."

Oh. For the second time since lunch, my belly feels hollow. "University."

The envelope makes a scratchy sound like he's clutching it tighter. Perhaps he senses that hollowness, because he drops his gaze. "Give me a minute, and we can crack out the video games."

Jace starts up the stairs, then stops and looks over the banister to where I'm still moping in the entryway. "It's still a year away."

coal

Ernie and Bert come for a sleepover. We've been playing computer games in the gaming room all night and it's close to two o'clock in the morning. The guys settle into their coal-colored sleeping bags on the floor and switch on the TV. "Something's always on at this time of night," Ernie says, flicking through the channels. "Bert, hit the lights."

The room is sucked into darkness and the TV screen becomes the focal point. I'm sitting on the couch above the two guys, gripping the arm. Soft grunts and moans fill the room and fill my ears. Bert and Ernie laugh and shove their hands into their bags.

Ernie looks at me, deadpan. "On the Mohs scale of hardness, I'm like a *ten*."

Their sleeping bags start jerking in the middle—

"Need to piss!" I leap up from the couch and hurry out. "Shit."

"Not having a good time?"

I jump. Jace is trundling back from the bathroom. Like me, he's in nothing but boxers and a sleeping shirt.

I shrug. "They're watching porn."

"Oh," Jace says, like it's the most natural thing in the world. "And?"

"Well . . . I don't know."

"You don't want to do it? That's cool."

"No, I do. But they—they've done this before. In front of each other, I mean."

Jace smiles. "You're nervous?"

That, and the porn they're watching isn't exactly what I would have chosen.

Jace bites his lip and comes closer. "Maybe you need to find someone you feel more comfortable with?"

I swallow and look down at us, close but not quite touching. With a shaky hand, I touch Jace's chest, then curl a fistful of shirt and draw him in close. He steps into it and his body presses against mine; warm, solid, smelling of soap and citrus. I swallow. "Are you offering?"

Jace laughs softly, the puffs hitting my cheek and skimming to my ear. He doesn't pull away immediately. "What if I am?"

Does that mean you're gay too? Or just horny?

He walks back into his room, leaving the door open. An invitation. Just under the skin it bubbles, and I even step up to the threshold of his room. He's holding the door, watching me.

"Just a jerk off?" I ask.

"What else would it be?"

His room is dark, but milky light seeps in at the cracks of his curtains. Jace shoves his messy bedspread back and pats the cleared space.

It's excitingly awkward. I'm hard, though, and watching Jace touch himself through his piano-key boxers is making me harder. Through the wall, muffled grunts and moans emanate from the TV.

Jace pulls out a small orange tub from his side drawer. A faint vanilla smell drifts into the air. "What is that?"

"This, my friend, is the best lube ever."

He grins and carefully pulls down his boxers, enough to expose his hard length. I've seen him before when he's dropped his towel on the way to the shower, but never when he's hard. He's not quite as long as me.

He grabs himself and pumps a few times. I shove my hand under my boxers and grab my cock. When I look up, he's watching me with heat and hunger in his eyes. He's as horny as Bert and

Ernie were. He's as horny as me—

Scooping up some of the lubricant, he leans over and whispers, "You have nothing to hide, Cooper. Be confident."

"My hand down my shorts is not confident enough for you?"

"I'm just saying. You're cool to be yourself in here. I'm your friend. You can trust me. And I trust you."

He drops back against the bed and slicks the lube over his cock, pumping slowly. He stares toward the ceiling but I want his gaze on me. I stand, yank down my shorts and dip my fingers into the cool lubricant. I rub some over my length, gasping, and then settle down on the bed next to him. Our shoulders touch, and his muscles quiver as he works his arm.

I jerk myself a few quick times and settle into the same rhythm as Jace, stopping every third stroke to thumb the head. I roll my eyes toward him. *Look at me!*

"Jace?"

"Yeah?" he says breathily.

"Swap cocks?" I let mine go and grab his. He's rock hard but his skin is silky. He gasps, then firmly wraps his warm hand around my stiffness. "That confident enough for you?"

I moan as the pad of his thumb moves over the slit at my head.

This feels too good to be really happening. I pump him faster. The lube is slick and—I can't help it.

I'm not going to last long.

Look at me!

He stiffens, body tensing. He grips me harder. I tense too, and we release with guttural groans and incomprehensible whispers.

Jace keeps his hand on my groin for a few moments longer, still staring toward the ceiling but with a contented smile quirking his lips. We let each other go and push up onto our elbows. Our stomachs are covered in spunk that smells like vanilla. I'll never think the same about vanilla.

I chuckle at this thought, and that's when I notice how quiet Jace is. The contented smile is gone and his expression is impassive. He sits up and rests his elbows against his knees and bites his bottom lip.

"Regretting the mutual jerk?"

"No," he says, simply. "I'm really not."

He sighs and grabs a warm washcloth for us. When we're all tucked back into our boxers, he looks at me and shrugs. "You heading back in there for another go with the boys?"

I'm not expecting this question, and it feels crass. But why should it?

Because it was more than a jerkoff for me.

"That was enough confidence for one night."

amber

I raid the liquor cabinet.

Dad and Lila are in bed but I'm not ready to do the same. Not yet, dammit. I'm sixteen, just finished mock exams . . . I'm going to stay up until midnight at least!

Jace too.

"What are you doing?" he hisses when I procure a quarter-bottle of whiskey.

"Grab two glasses and let's go to our balcony."

We sit against the semi-warm wall of the house, whiskey bottle resting between us, gripping our glasses and watching the last pink streaks fade from the night sky. The amber alcohol burns as it slips down my throat—it's how I imagine liquid amber should taste: like smoked wood and honey. It warms my belly and my veins.

I'm too sensible to take more than one decent slosh, and the fact is a little depressing. I never do anything crazy or wild. I'm a straight-A student who's never cut a day of school in his life. A guy whose only questionable behavior is hanging around Ernie and Bert and their filthy mouths. And mutually jacking off with a straight guy who is a few vows away from being my stepbrother.

Okay, so maybe I'm a little crazy.

I accidentally slosh whiskey over myself when I catch Jace looking at me.

"Boo," he says belatedly.

"Dickweed," I murmur.

He raises a brow. "Really, Cooper. And here I thought you were growing up."

I'm tipsy. I feel the giggle before it comes out. "I want to do something wild. *Do* something."

"Stealing Dad's whiskey isn't enough?"

"It's a start. But I want something to exhilarate me."

"Being with me isn't enough?"

An awkward beat passes. At least, I find it awkward because I think Jace knows how good I feel when we are close.

He's smiling at me, eyes twinkling.

It's a joke!

I laugh and quickly stand. "Let's go for a walk to the cave."

We duck in to see the glowworms but I'm too restless to be here long and I don't want to disturb them. I pull Jace out and drag him further up the creek. Walking in the bush at night lends a mysterious feel to the already eerie air.

We've probably walked the length of our street and are close to the local park. We stop at a pool in the river. Not the playground kind but the large-expanse-of-field-and-trees-and-river kind. It's quiet. Empty. A warm wind pushes us over the pebbly bank to the water.

On the other side of the river, a large rock face looms. A long rope hangs from a tree at the top of it.

Jace bends over and for a moment I think he's checking out our reflections, but he pulls at his laces and toes off his shoes. "You want exhilarating?" He grabs my laces too. "Then strip. We're going for a swim."

I laugh. "You can't be serious. It's cold in there. And dark. And what about eels?"

"Nothing will harm you." He peels off his shirt and throws it with his shoes behind him.

Moonlight touches his chest. A breeze pebbles his skin, making him appear wet though he's not finished undressing. The greenstone hook stands out against his lighter skin. I want to step closer, touch it—

Jace unbuttons his jeans and slides his thumbs under the waistband. He doesn't look at me as he pulls down his pants and boxer-briefs in one fell swoop. They pool at his feet and he steps out of them.

He dips his foot into the river but I'm not watching his toes ripple the surface of the water, or the way his calf muscles flex, or even his fine soccer-trained thighs. I'm riveted to his ass and the curve of his cock, hanging from under a small patch of dark hair. The cock I'd had in my hand; the one I'd pumped to release. "Yep. Cold, all right."

I jerk my head away. The whiskey must be working its magic on me because I'm stripping too.

Jace wades into the water, hissing at the cold. When he's waist deep he looks back at me. I'm naked and sinking into the pebbles as I step into the water. It's cold but I'm almost oblivious to that jolt because I'm experiencing a bigger one.

Jace is still watching me. His gaze zips the length of my body. He smiles and leans back against the surface. "Didn't think you'd do it."

I push into the deep part of the river, where the cool waters cloak my waist. "You don't think much of me, do you?"

I wonder if he knows I'm quoting him from that first Halloween. Wonder if he remembers it as vividly as I do.

Jace smiles and submerges.

He's hard to see under the water. Movement stirs at my side and something brushes lightly over my thigh. When Jace comes up again, he's behind me. Water stirs against my back and Jace draws in air. At my neck, I feel his words. They're cheeky at first but the twinge in his voice mellows. "I think plenty of you, Cooper."

I turn.

Water drips from his hair onto his nose and runs over the tip. We're standing close and the air seems to snap and crackle between us.

"Jace," I say quietly.

This is your moment to tell him.

He pushes closer, water lapping against my stomach. My heart hammers so hard against my chest I'm sure it's going to break a rib.

"Yeah?" He bites his lip for a moment and it's beautiful. "What's up, Coop?"

"I—I—"

My foot slips on pebbles and I topple into Jace, smacking his chest as I try to correct myself. Jace's feet slip and bang against mine again—

We fall and the water sucks us under. Our bodies slide together as Jace pushes against me to set us on our feet again. His arm leaves my waist when we are both upright. I splutter up the water I swallowed.

Jace's loud laughter echoes off the rocks and bounces off my skin. It tickles in a good way, and I start laughing too.

We splash each other and laugh hysterically.

We don't stop until something slithers around my ankle and Jace swears to God it wasn't him.

"Eel!" I bound for the riverbank.

Jace charges behind me, alternating between swearing and laughing.

"Maybe it's not an eel. Maybe it's a freshwater mermaid trying to pull you, her aquamarine treasure, to the depths where you belong."

"You researched my birthstone?" I ask as we struggle into our clothes.

"Maybe a little." He slips his T-shirt over his head. "Did you know aquamarine is thought to cure the poisoned?"

I do know this. I also know it's a beryl mineral and ranges from 7.5 to 8 on the Mohs scale—I like to think I'm an aquamarine in strength of soul and mind, but I fear I break too easily. "If you're ever poisoned, Jace, I'll kiss you better."

He laughs. I laugh.

We ride that wave home.

chert

When I wake up, I'm in my bed and Jace is plastered over my back. I can feel his breath falling in regular intervals on the collar of my T-shirt. His arm is around me but a touch lower than usual. My morning wood is practically poking his forearm and it feels great.

I wiggle down but I only make the situation worse. Now his morning wood is pressing against the back of my balls. So much for escaping to the bathroom without waking him. I roll my shoulder back so it hits his chest.

Jace jerks out of sleep, throwing his hands up so fast he bashes the greenstone against his teeth. "Huh? What?"

"We've got school," I tell him.

He rolls over to check the clock and groans. "Do we have to?"

"Yep. I'd rather get ready now than have Dad come in and yell at us."

Especially since we're in the same bed.

Not that anything's going on under the sheets, but it can't look good. What would Dad say? Would he freak out? Would he take it in stride?

It isn't like we're related, after all.

Jace leaps out of bed like I'm holding a hot prong to his backside, and zips to his bedroom. I pull my shit together and am ready a half-hour later. Jace leaves his room at the same time, stuffing a notebook into his backpack.

It's been a while, so I scowl at him.

He scowls back. And then it's off to school. Annie is away on a field trip so it's just us. I head to the bus stop and Jace stops me halfway down the driveway.

"Hide in the backseat and I'll drive you."

I bite my lip. He's snuck me out a few times, and every time it's an adrenalin rush. I freak out thinking he'll be pulled over. "Sure," I say, and head for his hatchback. Like always, we part ways at school and don't look back.

Ernie and Bert meet me in the gym with fist bumps and high fives.

Ernie slings an arm around my neck in a headlock. Bert yells out, "Who's got the Coop?" Ernie shouts back, "I got the Coop." Their voices echo in the locker room, eliciting sniggers from our classmates. With a playful shove, Ernie lets me go. We're dressing into sports gear when Bert pins a look to Ernie which can only mean they're about to gang up on me. I have a feeling I know what it's about. They want me to tag along at the school dance coming up. I've avoided it the last three years. Ernie and Bert gesture to all the guys in the changing room.

"Everyone's going to be there, dude. You gotta come to this dance. It's our second to last year of high school! We might actually get lucky this year."

Someone snorts and Bert narrows his eyes on the culprit. "Shut up, Frank."

"So will you?" Ernie continues, and Bert in his infinite wisdom adds, "If you don't, people might think you're scared of the girls. Or that you're a fag."

The last few years have proven their mouths are bigger than their ass holes for all the shit that comes out of them. But this is cutting close to home, and heat is rising to my cheeks. I stutter and stuff on a sneaker, yanking the laces tightly. I don't dare to look at them. *Put your other shoe on, tie it up, get into the gym.*

Ernie crouches to my level. His eyebrows look like one long black caterpillar. "Are you?" he asks quietly, and when I don't—

can't—say anything and work the second sneaker, he swears. "Shit, you *are*."

He hasn't spoken particularly loud but the guys in my class seem to have a gossip radar stronger than my grandmother's. The changing room grows eerily quiet. A few shuffles, someone zipping a bag, and the sound of feet as someone leaves, but the rest is mute. Ernie and Bert are staring at me but the other guys' gazes are fixed on the walls, the hooks, or the cubbyholes. Their ears strain, anticipating whatever's coming next.

I don't give it to them. Won't.

I stuff my clothes into my bag, push past Ernie and Bert, shove the bag into a cubby hole and walk out of there as calmly as possible.

No one says anything during gym. Near the end Ernie tries to grab my arm, but I shake him off. When it's time to change back into my jeans and long-sleeved T-shirt, I zone out until it's just me and the wood-paneled corner of the room.

English class comes next. Whispers stir, and guys avoid looking my way. Girls glance at me furtively, curious and sympathetic.

I scribble harder, concentrating on the text in front of me until the words pop out from the book and don't make sense. I'm living in a cocoon of heat, and I'm just wishing it to blow over. I never admitted anything. They don't *know*.

First break comes, and I hole myself up in the library. The whispers will stop soon. I'm not cool enough for this to be big gossip. By lunchtime, half my class will have forgotten.

But they haven't. Everywhere I look, someone looks back at me. My toes tingle with the first signs of panic but I steel myself against it. It's just a rumor. Stupid rumors. And no one is being a stupid dick about it anyway. At least not to my face. They all just leave me alone, give me a wider berth than normal, a berth that is swollen with their whispers. It's like the telephone game, where each whisper gets exaggerated, until *he might be gay* becomes *he loves to take it up the ass*.

Ernie and Bert are speaking in hushed tones at our brick

wall in the courtyard. Bert shrugs and gestures for me to come over there, but if I do, I'm telling them this is all their fucking fault. Then they'll have all the proof they need that they're right. I am a fag.

I grit my teeth, twist away from them, and scan the courtyard for a new place to sit.

My gaze falls on a familiar figure perched on a bench in the middle of the courtyard.

A skateboarder whizzes past me and jumps onto a low ramp, twisting and landing steadily.

My view opens up once more, and there's Jace sitting next to Darren and some other dude he hangs out with. Darren is talking to him, and the way he's hunched and leaning in has me holding my breath. Whispers louden and tighten around me like a rope. I can't move.

Jace frowns and glances over his shoulder toward Ernie and Bert. His mouth moves but I can't lip-read what he says.

A warm panic stretches up my calves like little shots of electricity. I want to retch.

Jace leaps up from the bench, and the pained expression on his face tells me he's heard the whisperings too. The way he swiftly moves toward me tells me more. Not only has he heard, but he knows it's true.

My throat aches and my vision blurs with tears. I struggle to blink them back. The sun makes the moon on Jace's shirt glint, and his eyes beg me not to run.

That's when I realize I'm reeling back from him. I'm not ready to have him know. Not like this. I shake my head. *Go away, go away, go away!*

When he keeps coming, I turn on my heels and run through the whispering courtyard, behind the back of the school, and over the soccer fields to the far corner, which is void of life and traps me with chain-link fences.

"Shit." I kick at the fence and it rattles.

Panic sweeps through me harder and faster. I need a stone. Need to calm down. I need a bloody stone!

My breathing is strangled and my chest hurts as I drop to my knees and feel through the grass for a rock, a stone—*something.* Blades of grass slice through my fingers as I comb the ground. My sight is blurry and a tear drops onto the back of my hand. I smear it on the grass and continue to hunt.

I grit my teeth shakily, to stop myself from doing any more of it. *Get it together. So what he knows? He was going to find out eventually.*

"Cooper!"

It's his voice. He's found me.

Like I didn't want him to.

Like I hoped he would.

He's across the soccer field, jogging over.

I search desperately for a stone, digging into the soil like it will unearth my peace. When it doesn't, I sit on my haunches and stare at my empty, dirty hands.

"Cooper," Jace says again, standing before me wearing a worried frown.

"I can't find one," I say. He drops to his knees in front of me, shuffles forward and pulls my hands so I'm kneeling too. He wraps his arms around me and squeezes me tightly.

"Are you okay?" he asks against my hair.

"Yeah, no, I mean, whatever, right? Just rumors."

He shakes his head.

"Fine," I say and draw away from him to search the ground. "It's true."

Jace breathes out heavily and helps me look. After a few minutes, he shakes his head. "Stuff it," he says and stands up, pulling me with him.

"What?" I say.

He balls up his fist and presses it into my open palm. "I'll be your rock. Do you think you can handle that today?"

I squeeze his warm fist. His pulse—or is that mine?—beats under my finger.

I'll never look at his hand the same. It will always remind me of this day, this humiliation, this anger, and this exhilarating wave I'm riding that's drawing me closer to something I've only dreamed about.

I need to be honest. I look up at him and swallow. "I'm sorry, Jace."

"Why? You haven't done anything wrong."

I shake my head. "I'm sorry because you weren't meant to be the last person to know, to be told by a bunch of losers. You were meant to hear it from me. I wanted to tell you last night at the river."

He sucks in his lips and nods before looking through the chain-link fence to the busy street. "You want to go home?"

"Cut school?"

"So what?"

"Okay. But I'm supposed to be at Mum's the rest of the week."

"I know," he says as we head across the field. "Let's go there then."

"So this is what your room looks like," Jace says, taking in the single bed, the desk littered with books, and the thirty toolboxes stacked against the back wall. I use the toolboxes to compartmentalize my rocks and keep everything in order. Each is labeled according to the month and year it represents, running all the way back to when I was two and picked up my first limestone.

Jace stands in the middle of the room, and I wonder if he's imagining me studying or playing computer games at my desk, trying and failing miserably to do push-ups on the round red rug, coming in wet from the shower with only a towel wrapped around my waist, jerking off to the thought of him under the bedspread—

You wish!

I turn on music to fill the silence but I keep it low so we can talk.

The springs in my mattress squeak as Jace sits on my bed. His reflection stares back at me from the photo I have of Mum, Dad, Annie and me that's on my desk.

"I have a confession," Jace says and I startle, standing up from my chair. It swivels in a full circle behind me before bumping against the desk.

"Confession?"

Jace bites his bottom lip and pushes off from the bed. He walks around the room, touching the dresser and studying the stones I have on display. He looks at me through the large square mirror above the dresser. "I wasn't asleep when you left my tent that night."

I pause. "What do you mean?"

"I mean," he says, turning around and leaning against the drawers, "I shut my eyes when you dragged your sleeping bag out. After a few minutes, I snuck out and . . . well, I overheard you and Annie."

"You were spying on me?"

He folds his arms and looks ashamed. "I was curious what you were up to."

"Curious?" I have no thoughts of my own, and I scramble to accept what he's telling me.

"I wondered what you were doing. I thought I might scare you for a laugh. Pounce on you or something."

"Pounce?"

Jace winces and chuckles. "Trust you to focus on *that* poor choice of word."

I don't know what I'm saying but I start speaking. "So there wouldn't have been any pouncing?"

Pushing off my dresser, Jace struts toward me. He shrugs as if he's answering his own question. "If you want there to be pouncing, there can be, okay? Plenty of it. In fact, let's start now."

Jace touches my chest and pushes me onto the bed. I barely process what's happening when he leaps on me, pinning me to the mattress. His greenstone slips out from the collar of his shirt and hangs at my throat. "So you're gay," he says, and this time I'm aware of what he's saying. I detect an undercurrent of anger. "Why didn't you tell me?"

Because it's you. You're the one I'm attracted to. You're the one that makes my heart go berserk.

When I don't answer, he rolls off me. I instantly miss his weight. Miss his focused stare boring into me for answers.

"As you can see, I'm okay with it. Did you think I wouldn't be?"

"No," I say, and it comes out croaked. What I really need to know is if I'm projecting feelings that aren't like *that*.

But of course they're not. I've seen his porn stash after all. He's told me he's interested in Susan. I can't even believe the warm lie that he's faking all that because he's afraid to come out—because why would he be? He's okay with me being gay, and he knows his parents are okay with it too. Nothing's holding him back. *Because he doesn't harbor any secret feelings toward you.*

I still want to ask. I want to know.

Don't destroy the illusion that he cares for you above and beyond a friend. You like imagining that one day he'll realize he wants you and ravage you like the hero in a corny romance—

"You can tell me anything. Just want you to know that."

We exchange looks. "I have nothing else to tell. That's it. My big secret, exposed. If you want to put some distance between us, I'll understand."

Jace sits up. "What the hell?"

"I just mean—"

"I know what you mean. You think I'm worried you're going to jump me?" He laughs. "You've had plenty of opportunity already. Why would things change now? Besides, the whole stepbrother thing."

I laugh. "Yeah. Stepbrothers." And because I can't help it, I add, "Not technically, though. Even if we were stepbrothers, it's not like we're related."

Jace's gaze flashes to mine, and his breath hitches. "I guess. Not really related. Not by blood." For a second, I think he's going to lean in and say something else, but he frowns and makes an abrupt change of topic. "I asked Susan to the dance. She said as long as I don't barf all over her, she'd love to go with me."

"Romantic." This comes out stonily.

Jace laughs. "You going this year, brother?"

Brother? What the hell is that? "I'm gay. Who would I go with?"

He shrugs. "You should go anyway. Stand up for who you are, show them you don't care what anyone thinks."

"Would you do that?" I ask. "If you were in my shoes?"

He's quiet for a long time. "Okay, maybe it's a stupid

idea. I just . . . But you're right. It's harder when it's yourself."

The front door shuts, and we scramble out of bed. "Mum's home."

"Should we hide?" Jace whispers. "Duck out the window?"

I smirk and open the door to the hall. "Mum?"

She appears a few seconds later, a bit flushed. Paul's lingering at her bedroom door, pulling nervously at his orange tie that matches his hair. He waves, accidentally flicking his tie into his face. He flattens it and silently laughs at himself.

"What are you doing home so early?"

"Kind of got outed at school. Needed to recuperate."

"Oh, dear. Should I make some tea?"

"Nah, I'm fine." For the most part. I glance from her to Paul. "Jace and I are going to get an ice cream and sit in the park."

"Are you sure—?"

"Yep." Her mouth twitches into a smile. She brushes past me and stands in front of him.

"This is Jace," I tell her, and before she starts wondering exactly why he's in my room, I add, "He drove me home."

"My God, you look just like Lila," she says.

"He's taller," I say as Jace says, "I'm taller."

We grin.

"You have her hair, eyes, nose, mouth, everything except how broad you are. That looks like . . ." She cocks her head and hums. "Well," she continues eventually. "You're one handsome guy."

"Mum!"

"Not as gorgeous as you, dear," she says. I groan.

"Just stop," I say. "Go back to the hunk in the hall."

It's her turn to redden. Now we're even.

When she's gone, Jace laughs. "Your Mum's all right," he says, and beckons me out of my room. "Now, I believe you said something about ice cream?"

alabaster

Ernie and Bert call me over the next few days. If I described what they wanted as a stone, it'd be alabaster, a translucent stone for forgiveness.

On the third day, I pick up the three-way call. I'm sitting on my single bed staring at my toolboxes. "What?"

"Dude, we totally screwed up."

"Bert-time," Ernie says.

"Shut up," Bert says. "You're not making this any better!"

"Fine. We screwed up big time. Better, Bert?"

"I don't know, ask Cooper."

"We're sorry. We were just surprised that you dig dudes. We don't care."

Bert says, "No, we don't care. Anyone who does care will see why I play defense."

"You gonna tackle them, Bert?" Ernie asks. "That imagery is so gay—hey, maybe you'll like it, Coop?"

"If this is your way of apologizing," I say. "You suck at it."

"We don't have much practice," Bert says. Ernie snorts.

"Yeah, because our big mouths have *never* gotten us into trouble before."

"We're sorry!" they say in unison.

"Come to the dance with us," Ernie says in a mischievous tone.

"Why?" I pick at the bed covers. Do I want to go? I thought I didn't but I am curious. It has nothing to do with knowing Jace will be there with Susan. Absolutely not. "People will whisper."

"Yeah, but they'll whisper anyway. At least you can control what they whisper about. Have the upper hand. Show them you don't care—and neither do your two incredibly hot, straight friends."

A pause.

Ernie huffs. "That was your cue to confirm our hotness. You know, from a guy's perspective."

Bert laughs. "Come on. He's way out of our league. We have ugly mugs."

"Speak for yourself—"

"Guys!" I shake my head. "I'll come but you have to suck up a little more before I'll forgive you."

"Did he say we have to suck him to be forgiven, Bert?"

"Ernie!" He's laughing, and I may be grinning as well.

kyanite

Jace is in a bad mood the next time I go to Dad's for the week. When I try to grab his arm and ask him what the matter is, he shoves me away.

I stumble onto the couch. Annie hisses in the background, flying out of her chair and abandoning her sewing machine.

"What the hell?" I push to my feet. "I just asked if you're okay! But obviously"—I shove his chest—"you aren't."

He grabs my wrists and yanks them to my side. His icy-blue eyes look like kyanite—one of the few blue minerals that occur naturally in this country.

"She's had enough bad luck! Sharing the love of her life for five years, losing the baby, getting a new family that barely tolerates her." He glares at Annie then stabs me with his gaze. "She doesn't deserve more!"

Annie steps between us, pushing against our chests until Jace swears under his breath and backs off. He leaves the gaming room with a slam of the door.

Annie frowns. "What was that about?"

I don't know, but I want to. I go after him but Annie grabs my sleeve and holds me back. "Don't. He needs time to cool off. He'll come to you when he's ready."

I snatch up my homework and take it to my room, pausing for a moment outside his door to hear the pounding bass of music. I pull out and rub the rare goodletite stone I found at the beach today. When I calm down, I place the goodletite on a shelf and settle in to do homework.

After not-concentrating on my biology for an hour, I take my *I'm a Rock Whisperer* cup and head off to make a cup of tea.

Annie stops me in the hall, twirling to display a purple skirt. "I sewed it myself. For the dance. What do you think?"

I nod. "Poufy."

She laughs. "You're not *that* type of gay, are you?"

"What type?"

"The—never mind." She glances at my cup. "Tea? Make me one too?"

"Make it yourself. I'm not doing the loose green tea, temperature thingy you like."

"If you boil the water it releases too many tannins and tastes bitter."

"Wow," I say, grinning. "You sound just like Mum right now."

She attempts a scowl but it morphs into a grin. "Fine, I'll make my own."

"In your poufy skirt?"

"Shut up. I'll see what Dad says. Probably has more to say anyway."

He doesn't. But that's because he's not listening to us. He's sitting at the end of the dining table staring at the vase of roses. His deep frown shadows underneath his eyes. He rests his elbows on the table and rubs his temples.

"Dad?" I ask, forgetting about the tea. I set my empty cup on the table and take the chair adjacent to him. Annie does the same on the opposite side.

"What's the matter?" she asks.

Dad blinks and clasps his hands together. "I'm glad you guys are here."

My heart beats faster. Jace is yelling at me again, shoving at my chest. "What happened to Lila?" I ask. "Where is she?"

"She's gone to bed. Wants some quiet time." He shifts in his chair. "She wants me to talk to you." His voice cracks and he clears his throat. “Lila had a mammogram.”

“Breast cancer?” Annie’s voice is weak.

Dad slides his clasped hands close to him. “Yes. The doctors found some abnormalities. She has a four-centimeter tumor, and the cancer has spread to three lymph nodes near the armpit.”

She’s had enough bad luck!

Oh, Jace. I’m so sorry.

And Lila. Shit. “Will she be okay?”

“Yes,” he says stubbornly. “She’s going to have chemotherapy to shrink the tumor and surgery to get rid of it. And we’ll all support her.”

He looks at Annie the longest. Tears run down her cheeks. She leaps from the chair and throws herself at Dad. “I’m so sorry. So sorry. For everything. I love you. I’m sorry Lila’s sick. I’ll help. She’ll get better.”

I hug him too.

I think of Lila sick in her bedroom.

I think of Jace curled up in anger and resentment on his bed.

“I love you,” I whisper. “I’m going to be there to support you.”

Dad drags my cup across the table. “Going to make some tea, were you?”

“Yeah,” Annie and I say together.

“Good. I could use some too.” He passes the cup to Annie. “You make it, love. You know how it’s done.”

I scowl.

They sniff out a laugh.

goodletite

Jace avoids me for two weeks. He shuts himself in his room like Annie used to. He doesn't participate in dinners, and I don't see him around at school—except once, when he had an arm around Susan.

He needs some time to cool off. He'll come to you when he's ready.

Why doesn't he come already?

The night of the dance arrives, and before Bert and Ernie arrive, I slip a folded note under Jace's door. I linger, crouched in the hallway, hand pressed to the wood for a few moments until I hear the sound of footsteps and rustling paper. I'm about to turn away when the door creaks as if Jace is resting against it. I lean forward, my head against the cool door too. "I'm sorry," I whisper.

Sniff. I'm not certain but I think I hear a murmur. "Me too."

"Jace, I—" The doorbell chimes, ripping me out of the moment. "Dammit."

I curse Bert and Ernie for their punctuality as I go downstairs to let them in. We move to the kitchen and I pull out three Cokes. Annie is pinning pearls to her hair. She swishes her poufy skirt and tells us to have fun. She prances off.

Bert attempts to whistle. "Damn, I thought I had it." He frowns and tries again but he gives up when he fails the second time. "Your sister looks hot," he says simply. Ernie doesn't say anything but his eyes had followed her too.

"Gah!" I cover my ears. Not something I want to hear.

Ernie drops a large paper bag onto the dining table as he claps Bert on the back. "Yeah, let's give up the wolf-whistling." He jerks his head to me. "Why aren't you dressed yet?"

Ernie and Bert wear matching black tuxedos sans tie, and shirts with wide fat collars. And they think I'm not ready? My black pants and white shirt will do very well.

"I am dressed." I set the Cokes on the table. "Drink?"

Bert looks at Ernie. "Guess you were right about him not being that type of gay."

"What?" I start, and Ernie hushes me.

"Don't worry, I'm not that type of straight guy, either. I picked something out for you. Put it on." He slides the paper bag to me. I steady a can before it knocks over. "Should be your size. Five-ten, right?"

I peer into the bag and groan. "We're gonna look like the Three Musketeers."

"The Three Best-Dressed Musketeers," Ernie says.

"It has a weird collar," I say, pulling out the shirt.

"Wait for it," Bert warns me, rolling his eyes.

Ernie asks, "Who are we at school?" I shrug. "That's right. We're nobody. And what makes us stand out from the crowd?"

"Not much?"

"Exactly. Doesn't matter how sleek our suits are because every other guy will look sleek too," he says, gesturing for me to hurry up. I pull off my shirt and slip into the fat-collared one. "To stand out, we have to do the unexpected."

"And these shirts are the way to go?"

"Hey, dude, you said it. Three Musketeers. Girls dig that shit."

I laugh. I may be gay but I'm pretty sure girls won't dig this shirt.

I wear it anyway. For laughs, and to keep Ernie placated. The rest of the suit feels smooth and silky. I find the goodletite I had in my other pocket and slip it inside the jacket's inner pocket. It creates a slight bulge at my chest but it's calming. I have a rare stone made of sapphire, ruby, and tourmaline; I'll be fine. Whispers can't hurt me.

A wolf-whistle slices cleanly through the air. All three of us look up as Lila waltzes into the kitchen with an amused smile and a camera. *Click. Click.* "Looking great, boys."

Ernie puts an arm around me, and Bert poses for the camera.

"At least one of you looks excited," Lila says.

To make things just a little better for her if I can, I join in with the posing.

She flips through some of the shots she's taken. "Your dad's going to piss himself when he sees these. Now boys, the embarrassing part. You're too young to have sex, so don't. And make sure your condoms aren't expired. Trust me, that would not lead to a good time. Now to find that son of mine."

She whisks out of the room and leaves us blushing.

"Dude," Bert whispers. "Lila is way thoughtful."

"And way hot!" Ernie adds. I throw him a look that makes him shirk behind Bert.

And way sick.

My chest suddenly feels tight. Jace is sniffing again.

We arrive at the dance an hour into it, which is great because the whole evening will be over and done with much faster.

It's everything I expect a dance to be: dark, flashing lights, terrible music. A group of couples dance in the middle of the converted gym but the majority of us are hanging in the corners or sitting at the tables. A few guys narrow their eyes in my direction and I sense their whispers in the air, but Ernie and Bert shield me.

A group of young girls snigger at us, and Ernie shakes his head. "They wouldn't be able to handle all this anyway."

Bert pulls out a flask he's smuggled in and hands it to his friend. A good swig later, it's passed to me. "Nah, I'm good." I lean against the back wall. "So this is it?"

"This is *it*!" Ernie repeats. "Do you see how short their skirts are? How full their racks?"

Bert sighs. "We're never getting laid."

“I repeat. This is it? Question mark.”

“All this and dancing as well.”

A fast, upbeat song launches an outbreak of grinding thighs and bumping hips. I’ve been scouring all the faces since I got here for any sign of Jace. Jace and *Susan.*

“Aaaaand,” Ernie says, squaring his chest and facing me. “This dance is going to be epic.” He bows slightly and extends a hand. “Cooper, will you dance with me?”

I snort and fold my arms. What is he doing? Is this some kind of joke? “That’s not funny.”

Ernie keeps his hand extended. “I’m not joking.”

I shake my head. “We can’t do that here.”

“Why not?” He drops his hand and turns to Bert. “Hey, want to show him how it’s done?”

Ernie leads Bert to the dance floor, and Bert twirls Ernie around. Ernie scowls and tries to spin Bert but Bert’s too tall for him. They laugh and boogie some more. They’re touching—at one point they’re even grinding—and they don’t care that people are staring. A few jerks mutter “fag,” and a few guys in the corner stick a finger down their throat but more people are smiling than anything—

Jace.

Dancing with Susan, arms looped around her waist. His suit makes him appear older, like he’s a future Jace. He’s everything I imagined he’d be—and more.

Susan runs her hand up the back of his hair, and I push off the wall, glaring at her through the throngs of dancers. I might have been able to handle it. Might have been able to shrug it off.

Except that Jace smiles at her and whispers something in her ear.

My throat tightens and a strange buzz fills me with energy. I weave to Ernie and Bert, who stop dancing when they notice my clenched fists.

“You okay, man?” Bert asks, puffing out his chest. “Someone bothering you?”

“I just—” Want to go home? Was that it? “—will you

dance with me?"

Ernie breaks away from Bert. "Thought you'd never ask."

It's strange when Ernie takes my hands and pulls me close. Awkward, and his aftershave overpowers me. But we manage something akin to dancing, and halfway through the second song, I relax as our laughter drowns out the whispers. So long as I don't look across the room to Jace, I'm fine.

I find my sister across the hall, watching us. Her head is cocked slightly and a mesmerized smile makes her face glow.

"Me too, me too," Bert says, butting Ernie out the way and grabbing my hips. "All the girls are looking. Share the love."

Bert is taller than me but not by much. I'm spin him around per Ernie's request.

"Fag!" some bastard says at the sidelines. I flip him the bird.

When Class A bastard says it again, Bert balls his fists and storms toward him. I grab Bert's shirt. "Just leave it. Probably a closet case himself." My words shut the dumbass up.

I smile. *See? I can stand up for who I am.*

I whirl around at the tap on my shoulder, ready to block a punch if I have to.

"Jace!" I search the crowds for Susan. "But I thought—"

"Can I cut in?" He says to Bert, who backs off with a grin.

The mirrored ball reflects squares of light onto Jace's face. I try to nudge a small smile from him, but he's not biting. Something lurks behind the depths of his eyes. I glance at our shiny black shoes.

He touches my forearm.

I glance up. "What will Susan think?"

He looks at Susan, who's sitting on a bench chatting with Darren and my sister. "It's fine."

His hand slides up my arm to my shoulder, and he steps closer. We're almost the same height. "I got your note."

The last of my jealousy bleeds away, replaced by a pulsing ache. "I am, okay? Always there."

"She's going to fight it. She will." His voice is stern, determined, as if he's convincing himself. "Now, just . . . dance with me?"

I swallow and fumble for a loose hold on his hips. His fingers press into my shoulder blades as he draws me nearer. Our auras hum, and our lengths are but an inch apart. His cheek brushes mine for a tender moment. "I'm sorry for shutting you out."

We sway slowly to the beat, but everyone else is jumping and swinging wildly.

A tear falls onto my neck and rolls under my collar.

I slide my arms around his waist and squeeze. "I'm here. I'll be here for whatever you need."

Another tear follows the same path. With every inch, my pain deepens. I don't know what else I can say. Don't know what else I can do.

So I say nothing. Do nothing.

Just feel the stone against my heart and pray everything will turn out okay.

And dance.

opal

Dad fumbles with his key, trying to open the damn door. Jace has an arm wrapped around his mum. The air is tense, pensive, as it always is after coming home from one of her treatments. The key sliding into the lock sounds like cymbals battering together. Then the key gets stuck, and Dad jiggles.

I rest a hand over my dad's trembling one, and take over. Lila burps softly as I push open the door. She makes it over the threshold before retching. A pained and embarrassed groan warbles her "Sorry."

Dad and Jace stroke her back as another spasm takes hold of her. Annie pales. "I'll . . . make some tea." She hurries away.

The acidic scent fills the entranceway and follows me to the cleaning supplies, where I grab a mop and then fill a bucket of soapy water.

When I come back to clean up, Jace grabs the bucket and mop. Twisting his back as if to curtain his mum from me, he cleans up. I back away. I feel so . . . so stupid. Useless.

I race upstairs and make sure she has a bucket by the bed and some water. Dad carries Lila to the bathroom first, and then settles her in under the covers. Jace stands with me at the door; his body is strung tight and he shifts from foot to foot, then pushes his fingers into his pockets. Pulls them out again.

Lila chuckles softly. “Knock-knock,” she says, looking at Jace and me.

Jace frowns. “Who’s there?”

“Cancer.”

His Adam’s apple bobs with quick swallows. “Cancer who?”

“Cancer see I need some sleep?”

Jace blinks rapidly, twists, and darts out of the room.

Lila swears, tries to call after him, but he isn’t coming back. “Too much, then,” she says.

Dad kisses her thinning hair. “He’ll be all right. You rest now, beautiful.”

She leans back against the pillows. “Just for a bit. Then I’ll talk with him.”

I awkwardly wish her a good sleep. I’m itching to find Jace, and race downstairs where Annie points out the kitchen window. I slip out the opened patio door, catching Jace in the back garden at the exact spot I bloodied his nose all those years ago. His shoulders spasm with a silent cry and then he hiccups. I fold him into a hug, and he clutches me so tight that I taste his fear. He sniffs against my neck and whimpers. “Don’t let go.”

* * *

A month later, Jace is at his piano, pounding out sharp, violent pieces, surging his anger into the instrument. Waiting. Waiting for Lila to come home.

The music snatches my breath, all the way from the kitchen where I sit with Annie, staring into my empty cup.

Annie lifts the teapot to pour me some more when the familiar sound of the door opening stops her. We edge out to the arched doorway, pausing there as Dad steps inside with Lila. They are both smiling today.

“Jace!” Dad yells, and the music stops abruptly. Seconds later, the stairs are groaning under his impatient gait.

Lila beckons us nearer and we flock to her.

“Things are looking good for surgery soon,” Dad says, and

kisses Lila's cheek with a smack. "We're positive about the progress. So are the doctors."

Jace steals closer and wraps his mum into a hug. Annie and I join in until we are one big lump of warm wishes. Jace twists his head and captures my gaze; the tension he's held over the last months is still there, but a hopeful smile brackets one side of his lips.

"I made some tea," Annie says as we break apart.

"That would be lovely." Lila and Dad follow her to the dining room.

"Cooper and I are going out for an hour," Jace calls to them. "Do you need anything?"

They don't.

Jace quietly gestures to follow him to the hatchback. Ten minutes later, we are strolling on the beach, enjoying the cool sand, beautiful seashells, crashing waves, shrieking seagulls, and the distant scent of fish and chips. Shells poke into my soles, assaulting me with sharp pangs that remind me I am not dreaming.

Jace picks up a beautiful paua shell. It shines as though the seas have been polishing it for decades, and the inside swirls with dazzling greens and blues.

"These are my favorite shells," he says.

He passes it to me and I take it.

"What's your favorite stone, Cooper?"

I laugh. "That's like a parent choosing a favorite kid or something."

"But what do you consider special? Diamond, maybe?"

"Diamond is the strongest, and I do like it. It's pretty much a stone of optimism. No matter how you turn it, the light is always there."

The shoes dangling from Jace's shoulder start to slip, but I catch them before they hit the sand. "However," I whisper, setting his shoes back on his firm shoulders, "my favorite stone is opal."

Found in Australia where an enormous inland ocean used to be, opal is literally like touching a prehistoric ocean. As the ocean dried out, water seeped into the earth's cracks weathering sandstone and making a silica-rich environment for my favorite stone to form.

"I know it's an Aussie stone," I say, grinning, "but don't hate me. I really like them."

Jace scowls. "Traitor."

"And greenstones," I add hurriedly before I'm revoked of my Kiwi status. "Of course."

He laughs and strokes his hook. "Next you'll be telling me your favorite animal is the Koala."

"Well . . ."

He shakes his head.

We continue the length of the beach. At the end, we dip out toes into the water. "Thanks," he says over a crashing wave. "For the walk. It helps. You help."

"Anytime."

'Anytime' comes a couple of weeks later. The night before Lila's surgery.

Jace sneaks into my room. "Cooper?"

I'm not asleep. My nerves and hopes won't allow me to shut my eyes. "Yeah?"

He grabs my foot through the bedspread. "I can't sleep."

I know. He's been playing a nervous piece on the piano for the last hour. It was originally jubilant and hopeful, but then it delved into something dark and desperate that made me cover my ears with a pillow.

"Come see the glowworms with me?"

It's the middle of winter, and a cold wind is howling through the gutters.

I peel back the bedspread anyway. Five minutes later, I'm fully dressed and slipping through the fringes of the bush with Jace.

Icy wind ruffles our hair as we trudge to the cave. The glowworms have left for the season, but our special spot remains tranquil. I leave my worries at the entrance and allow myself to breathe.

"I'm scared," Jace says. He's standing at the wall.

I slide up behind him and slip my arms around his waist, my forehead pressed to his neck. "She has good doctors, she's strong.

She'll pull through."

My head bobs in unison with his nod.

"It's not just about Mum," he says, so quietly that I barely hear him.

"What else?"

"Me. Susan."

I grit my teeth.

He continues, "I slept with her for the first time last weekend."

I want to move away, but Jace is tracing something over the back of my hand. "It was after Mum told us things were looking good. I felt so hopeful. So full of energy. She kissed me and I had this need to be close, you know?"

"Right." I pull away, but Jace snatches my hand, holding me in place.

"No, that's the thing. It *didn't* feel right. I felt—nothing. Nothing."

I release my breath slowly. "Why does that scare you?"

Soft pitter-patters of rain turn into a pelting torrent.

"Because it makes everything dark."

"Jace, you wouldn't ever hurt yourself—"

"No. That's not it. I got this mail, Cooper, and I haven't opened it because I don't want things to change, but things will change and—" He turns around. "It'll snuff out the last of the light."

He scrubs his face.

"God, I wish I'd never slept with her. Wish Mum wasn't sick. Wish I wasn't so afraid all the time. Wish I was strong like you. You don't care what anyone thinks and you stand up for who you are. I need to do that too. But I *can't*. Fuck, I sound so stupid right now. I don't even know what I'm saying. I haven't slept in forever, and . . . I don't know."

I lift his chin. Hundreds of comforting words dance on the tip of my tongue, but instead of speaking any of them, I whisper, "I love you."

The rain crashes hard on the foliage and splashes into the

creek. My breath fogs into the cold night air. "More than a friend, Jace," I continue. "I am totally in love with you."

* * *

The blaze in Jace's eye tells me he's shocked, but the small twitch of his lip indicates he's not entirely surprised.

He blinks and lets out a slow breath that mingles with mine. I'm still replaying the moment in my mind and trying to understand why I said it. It was the truth—is the truth—but it's the worst-timed declaration of love in all of history.

You don't tell a man you love him when he's in the middle of a family crisis. When his mum is hours away from surgery and he's emotionally frail. You don't show him a fragile emotion that you've cultivated and protected for years when he hasn't slept properly in months.

I don't care. Exhilaration burns through my veins. I've said the truth, and the secret anchor in my chest has lifted. I'm not taking any of it back.

I want to kiss you, Jace. I want to make love to you and hold you forever.

I swallow, daring to hold his gaze. Is he scrambling to make sense of this? Is he figuring out how to gently let me down?

I stand there forever, waiting. The rain splashes into the entrance, and a few drops land on my boot. Jace rests his head against the wall and shuts his eyes. "Coop," he finally says exhaustedly.

I don't want to hear what he has to say. I never want to know he doesn't feel the same.

I draw back but he grabs my hands. "Cooper, it's complicated."

Of all the things I expect him to say—*I don't see you that way, I love you too, you're just a stepbrother to me, I love you as a friend*—this is not one of them. "Complicated?"

A long stretch of silence passes. He starts to speak but stops. Twice. Then he manages to say, "You're my closest friend. I need that right now."

I nod. My mouth is dry and I'm shaking. I nod again and duck out of there. Rain hits my face and drizzles down my neck and under my jacket. At the edge of the creek, I find a speckled stone covered in wet moss. Conglomerate, maybe. I pocket it and let out a shuddering breath.

He needs me as a friend.

His mum is having surgery tomorrow.

I sniff, nod, then turn back to Jace and take him home.

laminae

I crawl into Annie's bed. She wraps her arms around me, no questions asked. Does she think I'm worried about Lila's surgery, or does she know it's more than that? How much does Annie know?

I grip my moss-covered stone and cry. She steers my head to her shoulder and pats my back. "It's okay, it's going to be okay."

Her shirt is wet with my tears. She passes me a tissue but I quickly have to grasp for another. When I'm finally spent of energy, I lie down on the pillow. "Sorry, Annie."

She rolls over and kisses my cheek. "Is there something more going on, Coop? I'm afraid for Lila too but it was Jace's name you kept saying."

I'm thankful for the dark, for the shadows that will hide the truth. "I feel for him," I say. "He only has his mum."

"Dad too."

"I mean *real* relatives."

"He has you and me, even if he does have poor taste in tea. But I'm used to that with you, so—"

"That's not what I meant."

"It doesn't matter that we don't share the same blood. We have two homes, and this is one of them. Jace will always be family now."

I curl onto my side. Annie's hair glows dimly despite the

dark. “How’d you go from hating them to loving them so quickly?”

“I didn’t say I love them.”

But she’s blinking back tears, and I know she cares.

“This is just the way it is. No one said you can choose your family, right?”

Suddenly it’s nine months ago, and Jace and I are in the cave: *I would have chosen you.* That was the moment I realized my love stretched beyond friendship. The moment that eventually led to tonight: *I am totally in love with you.*

“I would have chosen them,” I say. A pregnant pause, then a smile. “You’re right. We are forever now.”

“Even when things change,” Annie agrees.

Change. The word rings like a church bell on a Sunday morning, trying to stir my soul and snatch it.

Change is coming. Hell, it could be coming tomorrow. If not tomorrow then it will come in five months when Annie and Jace break away from the nest and fly on their own.

Of course, it’s to be expected. Time and the pressures of life make it necessary. Like basalt to granulite, mudstone to slate, limestone to marble, kid Jace will turn into adult Jace.

Kid me will turn into adult me.

“Do you know where you’ll go to university?”

She puffs up her pillow. “I think I want to study psychology and go to Victoria University. Vic has a great program.”

My broad smile cracks the dried tears on my face. “You’ll be staying in Wellington?”

“Yeah. I want to try flatting though.”

“Oh. Yeah. That makes sense.” *Please don’t leave me alone!*

“But I’ll come for dinner sometimes. You can hang wherever I’m living too.”

“Okay.” It’s not okay, really. But it’s all I have.

Will Jace offer the same thing? Or did I ruin it with my declaration?

I place the stone on the corner of the pillow between us. “I wish things didn’t have to change.”

Lila's operation to remove the tumor was a success, and a dark cloud has lifted from our house. Rays of sunlight stream through the windows.

Dad and Jace embrace in the foyer over Lila's hospital bag. Annie and I huddle in like we're rugby players. Like Jace, Dad looks ragged. He's barely slept the last months, and healthy eating hasn't been his biggest priority, no matter how much Annie and I nag him to stay fit.

"Thank you," Dad says. "Thank you for all being there. For showing us what a strong family we can be. I love you. I love you all very much."

We huddle amongst his words and love, then slowly break apart. Dad and Annie move to the kitchen for tea while I sneak upstairs to peek through Dad's bedroom door. Lila is curled up on the bed holding a framed photo.

Jace glides to his piano and plays bright, cheerful music.

Lila shuts her eyes and breathes it in. She smiles.

The light is back.

ironstone

The days fly by with school and the routine of home life.

The nights, however, are long.

Too much time to think, to hope, to despair. The women I love are shining brighter than ever. Lila, with new strength and spirit; Mum, with passion and adventure; Annie, with bright confidence and maturity. They seem older, wiser, *happier.*

But I'm not happier. I wonder if Jace has forgotten our last moment together. He's never brought it up, and he hasn't changed his behavior. He still steals me away and drives us to the beach to pig out on ice cream. He still laughs at my Bert and Ernie misadventures. He still finds rocks and stones for me. He still wraps an arm around my neck as we walk barefoot in ocean tides.

Twice, he's even crawled into my bed when he couldn't sleep.

But not a single word about that night.

I ponder Jace's silence as I line a fake coffin with red velvet in preparation for Dad's Halloween birthday.

Jace is supposed to be showing Annie the best keys on the piano for a haunted house tune, but he's playing Rocky Horror Picture Show's *Time Warp* instead.

"Madness takes its toll," he sings, his low pitch prickling my skin.

Annie joins in but the music stops when Dad clears his throat.

Lila slips her hand into Dad's, barely containing her smile.

"We have some news."

Jace clutches the edge of his piano stool so hard his knuckles go white.

"Good news," Lila says and bites her lip. "Doctors say I'm good."

Jace leaps off his chair. "You're good?" He hugs her before I can comprehend what she's said. Tears rim her eyes, and that smile finally breaks loose. "I'm good!"

Later in the evening, after the festivities, I find Jace in his room clutching an unopened brown envelope.

"What's that?"

"Nothing. Just something for university."

He hides it in his desk drawer.

I sit on the edge of his desk.

"Where are you going for university?" I ask. We've avoided the topic for months, but now that Jace has graduated, we can't hide from it any longer.

I hold still.

"I . . ." He looks down at the rip in my jeans. "In some ways I want to stay in Wellington and go to Vic."

"In some ways?" His words make me shiver.

He closes his eyes. "But I applied to Otago last week and got accepted."

I cannot make a coherent thought. "Dunedin?"

He nods.

"Your mum and dad know?"

"I told them to keep it quiet." He opens his eyes. "I wanted to tell you myself."

"So it's six weeks and goodbye?"

"We can talk on the phone. I'll be back for winter holidays and Christmas."

Only twice a year?

I exhale slowly. My belly feels hollow, and I want to throw up.

I leave his room and hurry outside. The path jars my every step thanks to the thin sandals I shoved on. Jace shouts from our balcony. I want to ignore him but I traipse over the moat toward him, cutting an angle to the side of the house. “I’m sorry,” he says, leaning over the rail.

I shrug. I need to get out of here. “Yeah, yeah. Hey, can I borrow your car?”

Jace leaves and returns with his keys, which he stuffs into an envelope and seals with a swipe of his tongue before handing to me.

I don’t open it until I’m at his car. Leaning against the roof, I pull out his keys, and then the note.

Forgive me.

I’ll miss you. Stay strong.

Sorry it’s not an opal.

I tip the envelope upside down, and a small stone tinkers onto the top of the car. Not much bigger than my thumbnail, a teardrop of matted red and black ironstone.

I clutch it tightly before carefully sealing it into the envelope and slipping it into my pocket. I hop into the hatchback, and drive.

And drive.

And drive.

garnet

Dad and Lila left for a long weekend getaway to a beautiful beach in Brisbane. After the year they've had, they deserve the break.

I convinced Annie to stay at Mum's for the four days. Quality time, I said, to do girly nights and female fraternizing.

The truth is, Jace and I want the weekend alone.

Time is winding down. After this weekend, we only get one week to live together. We're on the precipice of change, and we want to spend the last moments together, pretending we're not going to fall.

We get up early to hike the town.

On the last stretch to Oriental Bay, I find a flawed fragment of garnet and run its sharp side along the pad of my thumb.

"Let's have a look," Jace says, stealing it from me and holding the red stone up toward the light. "Fool's ruby?"

"Garnet."

He throws it toward the paua-blue sky that is streaked with long, wispy clouds, and it tumbles back down to him like a bloody raindrop. "And?" he says, catching it, a stupid little grin quirking his lip. "Surely you know more than that?"

I knock into his side as he throws it up again. I miraculously catch it as Jace stumbles, spraying sand in arcs toward the frothy tide.

"It's a stone of truth," I say to my fallen friend, extending an arm. He's laughing as he takes it.

"Really?"

"It helps release it." We make our way up the boulevard toward the café where Annie works. "Sometimes the information learned is painful but the garnet ensures that those truths are what the seeker needs to know." Jace stops walking and I turn back to him. The curious frown etched between his brows is the same single line that Annie has when she's unsure and a touch uncomfortable. "You all right?"

Jace folds his arms over his cassette-tape T-shirt, and I wait for him to speak. He stares at my hand encasing the garnet. "If you don't learn a truth, does that mean you don't really need it?"

I throw him the stone and he's quick to catch it. "I don't know." He catches up to my side and we continue to the café. *Garnet also increases sexual intimacy.*

With a sneaky smile, Annie serves us extra mini-muffins with Jace's coffee and my tea.

"How's quality time with Jace going?" she asks when Jace goes to the bathroom. "He's really turned out to be more than a brother hasn't he?"

I freeze and set down my tea before I spill it. "Wh—what?"

"I mean, you guys are like best friends. I'm sorry you're breaking up." She winks. What does that mean? "But it's only for a year, right? Then you can study down there with him."

Across the café, Jace is rounding tables, heading back to us. He winks, and everyone including my sister disappears.

I'm already planning to move to Dunedin. Just so I can be with you.

"So I was thinking," Jace says, sitting back down and watching Annie leave to serve another table, "after this, maybe we could shop for some music? I'd love to get my hands on a few more compositions."

I sip my tea with a shaky hand. "Yes. Of course."

* * *

After the music store, I take us out to dinner at a restaurant on the boat where we ate for his seventeenth birthday. I secretly hope it will rekindle Jace's memories of the cave that day, when I gave him the hook.

I'll never take it off.

We sit by the window overlooking the ocean. Jace touches the hook as if he knows what I'm thinking about, a fond smile playing at his lips.

Still wearing it.

A waiter lights the tea candles between us. Jace and I blush, shift uncomfortably, and stare out the window, which partially reflects our faces.

I wait a beat before I glance at his image. My heart jumps when I find he's looking at mine, and we're thirteen and fourteen again, standing at the bus stop, peeking at each other over our books . . .

Are we nearing the end of our duel?

My mood crashes and I spend the rest of the dinner paying too much attention to my seafood ravioli.

When we arrive home, I yawn even though I'm not tired. "I'm going to crash."

Jace frowns and stops me on the stairs. "It's only ten." He places one hand next to mine on the banister, and he tugs my fingers with his other hand. "Something's up."

"No. I'm fine." Sad. So fucking sad.

"Let me play you a new piece before you go to bed?"

I swallow. Nod.

In the gaming room, he perches himself on the piano stool. A single lamp offers just enough light for him to read his music.

I lean against the wall. Music beats against my skin and speeds up my pulse. Jace is completely focused on the music, an endearing frown etched between his eyebrows. When he finishes, he stares at the keys and smiles.

"Not bad," I say.

"Not bad?" He shakes his head. "I've never played that before. It was bloody perfect."

A trace of the grin I'd lost reappears. "Play something else. Sing."

"Sing?"

"I like it when you sing. You've got a good voice."

"What do you want me to play? I can do a couple of U2 covers."

"U2?"

"Mum's favorite. I learned a few when she was sick."

I move to the stool and sit next to him facing away from the piano, giving him just enough space to play. "Okay," I say. "Play one for me."

His Adam's apple juts out in a hard swallow, and his gaze sweeps over my face. "For you," he says slowly. A slight tremor passes through me.

He focuses on the keys, running his fingertips over them.

Then he starts.

I want to cry, want to laugh, want to curse him for making every hope swell to a breaking point. I know this song—Lila and my mum love it.

Now I love it.

When he sings the word *diamonds*, he smiles at me.

All I Want Is You.

I can't look at him, but I can't pull away. I silently beg for him to stop, but I wish he'd go on forever.

He remembers what you said to him that night. He never forgot.

I try to keep my tears back but they seep through my eyelashes.

Jace says *diamonds* again and his voice breaks. He stops playing. "Cooper?"

My voice is hoarse. "Yeah?"

He looks up, touches my cheeks. "Cooper—"

He kisses me.

His lips scrape over mine like a whisper. I freeze for three quick beats of my heart, and then we're frenzied. Fast, urgent, needy. He brings one hand to my neck while his other hand caresses my arm. His tongue meets mine like a drowning man fighting for oxygen. He tastes like the caramelized sugar on the crème brûlée we ate at dinner. His kisses leave my mouth and find my jaw, my neck, and—

My hands have found their way under Jace's T-shirt. His skin is hot, the planes of his back smooth and hard.

I want to explore more but the damn stool is making it difficult. As if reading my mind, Jace stands, pulling me up too. He steers me around it, leans on the piano so the higher notes clunk, and draws me fully against him. No inch between us. No question of where this is going.

He kisses me again, and breathes me in. My lips tingle as the air moves. His blue gaze is heavy as if he's probing me deeply. We are kissing again, his hands pulling at my T-shirt. I move back an inch to take it off and remove his.

I run my tongue down his neck and nibble at his collarbone before sinking to tease his nipple. He arches and a satisfying moan slips from him, stirring me to taste every inch of him.

I'm harder than I've ever been, and each time our groins mesh, he pumps me with desire. Need.

More.

Now!

I fumble to undo the buttons at his fly. Jace's breath hitches as I cup him through his boxers, and he nips my ear and works my jeans. Our pants shimmy to our knees, followed by our boxers. Jace kisses me again and I take hold of his cock like in my fantasies. His groan vibrates over my lip. The piano keys tinkle as he pulls me closer and takes my cock.

Look at me!

This time he does, and he pumps slowly, like he wants this to last forever. He licks his lips, then releases me and gently removes my hand off him. Our cocks touch and I press closer to rut against him as our fingers entwine.

The piano keys produce a cacophonous sound that mingles with our moans and heavy breaths. We ride the wave drawing us closer and closer—

"Cooper," he moans in my ear.

I cry out, orgasm shuddering through me, and a few seconds later Jace releases too.

"I . . . I . . ." Jace throws his head back as he catches his breath, and when he look at me again, his expression unnerves me. "Jace?"

He hesitates, then kisses me once more. It's slow, languid—a goodbye kiss? I grip him harder, kiss him harder. I don't want him to leave me. Ever.

He draws back and touches my lips. "I'm sorry."

The ache and shock of his apology startles me. I jump back, and Jace slips from my grasp.

He comes back, pants buttoned, holding a warm cloth for me, but something's different. When I'm cleaned and dressed again, I face him.

I stride over to him. "Why are you apologizing?" *That was the most touching moment of my life.*

"Because . . . because . . ."

"Because what?"

He turns away but I don't let him go that easily. I follow him into his bedroom. "Talk to me, Jace. Please, for God's sake, talk to me."

"I'm sorry because I shouldn't have done that. Not with you."

"With me?" I laugh but I'm far from amused. "Because I'm gay and you're not?"

He swears under his breath, then yanks out the brown envelope from his desk drawer. "No."

The envelope looks darker now. More ominous.

Jace slaps it on the desk between us. "Because you might be my brother."

"Might be?" My mind refuses to piece together what he's saying. "We're *step*brothers," I say. "We're not really related. We aren't even stepbrothers! We're just guys who met as teenagers and spent every second week together."

Jace slides the envelope toward me. "I want to convince myself." I stare at the envelope. Jace says, "I did a discrete DNA test of me and Dad."

My breath whistles in sharply. I shiver. "But you haven't opened it. You don't know for sure we're"—my stomach flips—"brothers."

Jace swipes away the tears in his eyes.

I lean against his desk, the corner of the envelope nudging my forearm.

"Why . . . how . . . what . . ."

He knows what I'm trying to ask. "Do you remember that night I was playing the piano and you burst in here, full of energy, and danced like you didn't have a care in the world?"

When he came over and began tickling me on the couch. I breathe in sharply; it's not a moment I can easily forget.

"I remember," I say. "Annie came in and told you your mum was crying."

"I went downstairs," Jace says, staring at the envelope. "Mum and Dad were having a fight."

"You said you didn't know why she was upset."

"I lied." He leaps up from his seat and paces the length of his bed. "They were arguing about getting married. Mum wanted to. Dad didn't. Mum tried to convince him. Said they were together after Dad broke up with your mum, before he learned about the pregnancy."

Jace slumps on his bed, clasps his hands together, and jiggles his leg. "Mum said 'I knew then you were the one. Thought you felt it too. Thought you would marry me.' And Dad said, 'For thinking I was the one, you sure moved on quickly!'"

I fold my arms against a shiver.

Jace continues, "I knew what Dad was digging at, that Mum quickly got pregnant with me. Dad pushed her again. 'What was his name, Roger? George?' And Mum said nothing. Nothing." Jace shakes his head. "I didn't know what to do but it made me miserable. You told me to do something about it so I had his toothbrush tested."

"The day you gave me that peach stone with the white wave." I recall him throwing the stone to me in the hall, the toothbrush in his other hand.

I close my eyes.

The air stirs, and Jace's shadow falls over me.

"Why didn't you open it?" I ask. I count his breaths. One, two, three. "Don't you want to know if he's your real dad too?"

One, two—"Not as much as I want to know he's not."

I open my eyes. Jace is staring at our feet, but he's standing close like he's torn between two emotions.

Like he's always been, hasn't he?

It's complicated.

Brothers.

I feel sick. "Open it."

Jace picks up the envelope. "I can't."

"I'll do it, then." His expression crumbles and I think he might cry, but he schools his emotion and passes me the envelope.

I thumb the edges. A small flap at one corner scrapes my skin—this is how far Jace has come to opening it. How many times has he stared at it and wondered? How many times has he tried to rip it open but shoved it back into the dark drawer?

How many times has his stomach flipped like mine is now?

What if it isn't a match? We could continue exploring our feelings for each other and be everything we want.

I could take him in my arms and kiss him so damn hard. I could push him onto his bed and love him all over again.

What if it is a match?

I stop thumbing the envelope.

Shake my head.

I can't either.

It's too risky.

I'd rather be in the purgatory of love than the hell of loss.

I drop it back in the drawer Jace pulled it from and slam it shut.

"Are you mad?" Jace asks after a long time. "For our moment? I know I shouldn't have, but . . . it's true. The song. I don't know what it makes me, but it's true. I'm disgusted with myself. I knew better. I shouldn't have. God, I'm so sorry."

Don't be. It was special. "For all we know, we're not related."

And if you are related? Do you really care? My stomach twists at the voice.

It'd be icky. It'd be proper incestuous. No more reassuring myself that my feelings are okay because we're not real siblings.

I bow my head.

Do you really care?

onyx

I don't see Jace the next time I'm at Dad's. He took an earlier flight to his new life, so it's just me and Annie and Jace's ghost at the dinner table with Dad and Lila.

I want onyx. Not to release the sorrow or grief.

But to become invisible.

To be a ghost alongside his.

part three: metamorphic

metamorphic: altered form.

amphibolite

Harder than limestone, heavier than granite. I feel like amphibolite.

The school year starts slowly, every day dragging longer than the last. Only the teachers are happy—my work is getting more elaborate and difficult. After my geology teacher submitted my essay to a lecturer he knows at Vic, Professor Donaldson wrote me a personal message informing me that she wants me to study in her department and, if I need it, she'll write me a letter of recommendation to the dean of admissions. Not that she thinks I'll need the help.

I won't. Not only is schoolwork the only distraction I have and what I pour everything into—I won't need the help because I don't want to stay in Wellington.

I shuffle alongside Ernie and Bert and hide in the protection of their laughs and jokes.

"Dude," Ernie says, punching my arm. We're at our spot in the courtyard, the brick wall. "Can you drive us to Annie's after class?"

I raise a brow. I know what he wants but I can't find the energy to care. "Her flatmates aren't interested." At least, I don't think they're interested. I haven't exactly been paying attention.

He and Bert exchange confused looks and shake their heads at each other. Ernie mouths, "What's up with him?"

"He seriously needs to get laid," Bert says, then clicks his fingers. “Got it. My cousin totally digs dudes too. He’ll be down for my birthday in a couple weeks.”

Ernie rubs his hands together. “Sold. Then maybe we’ll have the real Cooper back. Yeah,” he laughs. “Your cousin can pump some life into him.”

I’m drawn into the moment long enough to say, “Who says I wouldn’t be the one doing the pumping?”

“That’s our boy, though slightly more crass. I *like* it.”

I stare at the bench in the middle of the courtyard.

The bell rings, signaling our trek to class. The air feels different, thicker and stodgier.

After school, I find a large dark stone near the hatchback Jace left behind for me. When I pick it up, I don’t feel the weight of a thousand memories. I feel hollowness. Sympathetic hollowness, perhaps?

Bert and Ernie catch up. Arms sling around my waist and neck as they plead.

“We’ll be on our *best* behavior.” Ernie flutters his lashes. I’m about to say *no, not today*, when my pocket vibrates to life.

A gentle breeze carries the sharp taste of exhaust fumes mixed with Indian spices. Bert and Ernie’s sudden laughter rings in my ears.

The phone vibrates again, sending shivers racing up my arm as I take the call. “Jace!” A smile pulls my lips wide, and I laugh, twisting away from Ernie and Bert. The sun shines on my face and I breathe in the brightness. “How are you?”

His voice is croaky and he coughs. “Sorry. Autumn cold.”

“That sucks. You’re calling early this week.”

“Yeah, I’m going hiking this weekend so I wanted to say hey now.”

“Where are you going?” *And with who?*

“A couple of mates and I are doing the difficult trail at Kepler Track.”

“Mates?”

Jace knows me too well. “Cooper,” he says quietly. It’s a warning. It’s a plea. Please don’t go there. Let’s not talk about the bloody elephant in the room. Let's pretend it doesn't exist. Let's pretend *All I Want Is You* never happened.

Pretending is the unspoken rule of our weekly chats. Pretending is a different version of the duel we began on opposite sides of the street waiting for the bus. This time he's on the South Island, I'm on the North, and we are masters at pretending.

He pretends not to care about my love life, and I pretend not to care about his.

"What are you doing this weekend?" His play is shrewder.

Walking barefoot across the beach collecting paua shells for you and stones for me. "Nothing."

"Hey, I'm eighteen now. Want me to send you my driver's license? I can claim I lost it and get a new one."

"You want me to sneak into gay bars in hopes of getting lucky?"

Jace coughs again. "No." His voice cracks. "I just want you to have fun."

"I'd never get away with your ID. We look nothing alike."

"It's not healthy." Long pause. "Doing nothing."

So some rules are okay to break but not others?

He changes the subject, "How's the hatchback doing?"

"The only thing around here running smoothly."

"Fuck."

I curse myself for my lack of subtlety. "How's your music coming along?"

"Doesn't sound the same as it does at home. The pieces are more complicated but I'm pulling through. Getting better."

"Maybe you can play me something when you come home for the winter holidays?"

He coughs but doesn't answer. Voices call his name in the background. "Look," he says. "I gotta go. I'll call next week, okay?"

"Yeah, okay. Have a good hike."

"Do something this weekend, Cooper. Please?"

I glance over my shoulder at Ernie and Bert. "Promise."

When he hangs up, I hold the phone for a long moment

before facing the boys. "All right," I tell them, jingling the keys in my bag. "Let's go see Annie."

* * *

Annie's flat looks as though a bomb exploded in it. Crusty dishes are piled in the sink, heaps of clothing are thrown all over the floor, empty wine bottles give the air a sour bite, and the bathroom walls are edged with mold.

I decide to wait rather than use the bathroom.

"I thought girls were meant to be the clean ones," I say as she clears a space on the couch for us.

Annie shrugs. "There's only so many times you can bitch at your flatmates to clean up before it gets awkward."

I shake my head. "No wonder you're coming to Mum's for dinner more and more."

Ernie and Bert lounge in the mess like it's their throne. "Couple of beers, and we're set."

"Someone say beer?" One of Annie's flatmates walks in with a six-pack in one hand, and a bunch of shopping bags in the other.

Bert stares at the door like it's magical. "Couple of girls, and we're super set."

The girls hit it off with Bert and Ernie while I zone out of the conversation and think about Jace. My sister digs her fingernails in my arm and drags me to her room, which is surprisingly much cleaner than the rest of the house. We sit on the wide windowsill overlooking a weedy garden. "What's up, Coop?"

"Nothing. I'm . . . fine." Before she pushes further I ask about her. "How'd your date go with what's-his-name?"

She groans. "Steve. The one night wonder." A shrug. "Never do that again. Worst walk of shame ever. I banged into Darren looking like a prostitute." She blushes. "He had to know. All I wanted was to slink home and hide."

"Sorry."

"Yeah. But of course the one that got away will catch me at my worst."

We're quiet but Ernie and Bert are laughing in the background.

Annie pinches my arm. "You at Mum's this week?"

I shake my head. "Dad's. You coming for dinner this weekend?" It makes it easier when she comes, and I suspect that's why she makes more of an effort.

"I mean, I wasn't planning to. Tomorrow I'm watching this theatre production Chrissy is in. And I have group-project meeting on Sunday. But I don't have to see the play. Sure. I'll come out—"

"No, don't." I put on an extra cheery smile that tastes like cardboard. "I'm good. Next week, maybe."

"You sure?"

"Yeah, course."

"Invite your friends around. You guys could have a slumber party."

I haven't had Bert and Ernie sleep over since that night with Jace. I'm afraid if I do, all I'll remember is touching Jace the first time. Willing him to look at me.

Just a jerk off?

What else would it be?

"Yeah, they're busy. But I have a test to study for."

"You study harder than anyone I've met at university. You know where you're going next year?"

"Otago."

Dunedin.

Jace.

Do you care?

No. And I'll convince him not to either.

And the rest of the world if I have to.

Bert and Ernie are having a great time, so I leave them to it. They can catch a taxi home. They're too high to care I'm ditching them, anyway.

I drive the hatchback around the bays, driving and driving, until the sun finally sets.

"Cooper," Dad says when I finally get in the door. He and Lila are dressed up. "We were about to head out to dinner. Do you want to join us?"

"Nah, I'm good. I'll just hang here."

Lila unclips her earrings. "We don't need to go out. We'll hang with you."

Dad exchanges a look with her, and toes off his shoes. "Ordering in it is."

Despite their efforts to make the big house seem less empty and less quiet, it makes it worse. There should be more voices, more spark in the air.

I eat a few slices of pizza, fake a few yawns, and head upstairs.

The gaming room is dark, the piano sitting untouched for months. I sit on the stool and let the chill creep over me. If I close my eyes, I hear his song and his ghost settles around me as if pulling me into his arms.

I scrub my face and laugh at myself.

Then I go to bed. His bed.

greywacke

A week later when I'm at Mum's, I get mail from Jace. A greywacke stone that's broken on one side, and a short note.

From the Kepler Track. (The trail is beautiful.) This stone made sleeping impossible. It kept digging into my back, so I snuck out of the tent in the middle of the night, lifted the pegs, and pulled it out. Still couldn't sleep, though. After that, all I could think about was rocks.

I smile, and suddenly I'm *me* again.

We're apart but nothing has to change. This is just a test we'll pass with flying colors.

I hole myself up in my room, lie on the bed facing my toolboxes, and phone him.

It's so easy. He tells me about all the crazy people he's meeting in Dunedin and how I would love it down there.

He laughs. I laugh.

I make him take me to his dorm room and play something on his new piano. He asks me if he should sing, and I catch my breath.

He plays, and even through the phone it's beautiful.

We talk for over an hour. I never want this to end but my phone is beeping with low battery. Jace laughs again and tells me to have a good night.

I hang up, clutch the phone to my chest and bite my lip—

"Who was that?" I leap to my feet. Mum is leaning against the doorframe; the door mustn't have been closed properly. "Your boyfriend?"

I splutter. "Wh—what makes you think that?"

"You sound happy. Head over heels. I haven't heard you this animated in months."

I slip the phone in my pocket. "Dinner ready?"

"It *was* your boyfriend then? When do I get to meet him?"

Dread and nausea wash over me, and I finally understand why Jace has distanced himself.

"It was just a friend," I tell her. *Would you hate me if you knew I was in love with my maybe brother?* "Just a friend."

"Oh, unrequited, is it? That's a hard one but you have to hold out for someone special. Someone who wants you as much as you want him; someone who'll be proud to call you his boyfriend."

We have a roasted-chicken dinner, and Annie comes too. Paul, sitting opposite from Mum, opens a bottle of white wine and pours us each a glass, mine slighter than the rest but I don't care for alcohol anyway.

"What's this for?" Annie asks, glancing between Mum and Paul. Annie silently asks me with her facial expressions what this is all about.

I shake my head.

Mum stands up. "Good news," she says, smiling at Paul. "We're moving in together."

topaz

Winter comes.

Jace doesn't.

He has the chance to play a few gigs, so he won't be home until Christmas.

I call him to make alternate plans.

"I'll come down," I say as soon as he picks up. "Can take a flight tomorrow. I'd love to watch your gigs."

"Cooper," Jace says. His tone sounds distant. "You don't have to."

"I want to."

"I'm going to be in rehearsals most of the time. You'll be bored."

"I see." And I do, clearly. My eyes sting and my throat tightens.

Jace quickly changes the topic. "But hey, what's new? How's Annie?"

"Same old. She's fine. You?"

"Tried this fish and chips place near campus, it was great."

"Better than the one we go to here?"

"Different."

"So not better?"

"Cooper! Fuck. They don't use canola oil to fry the fish."

"We never asked what they use here. Could be coconut, maybe."

Silence.

I sit on the end of his bed and wish I had something else to say. But I don't. Neither does he.

A male voice speaks in the background, and Jace answers, "Just my brother. Be there soon."

Just my brother.

My stomach twists.

"Sorry," I say hurriedly. "Bert and Ernie just showed up. We're hitting some clubs tonight. I gotta . . . yeah. Later."

I barely give him the time to say goodbye before hanging up. I rummage for some topaz, hoping it will cure me from the deep madness creeping into my mind.

* * *

I'm not expecting Jace to phone me the next week, but when he doesn't, I curl into his bed and let the tears fall.

The edge of the pillow is wet. I shift, wiping my nose with the back of my hand. Lila startles me when she plops onto the edge of the bed and pats my back. I didn't even hear the door open. "Hey. Cheer up, love."

I roll onto my back and throw an arm over my face to hide my tears. "Lila."

Please go away. Leave me alone.

"Oh, darling." She touches my hair. "This has gone on too long. It hurts to see you so depressed."

"I'm not"—sniff—"depressed."

I stiffen as I realize I'm in Jace's bed. What is Lila thinking?

"It's hard being the one left behind, isn't it?"

A gurgling sound escapes as I try to stop my tears.

She strokes my hair, making my tears leak faster.

"I felt like that when your Dad left for America in my last year of school, too. He was my best friend. I cried and listened to a lot of U2, wallowing in my misery. It was tough going from hanging every day to nothing but the occasional call."

I nod.

"I miss Jace too. He grew up too damn fast."

"Do you cry and listen to U2 now?"

Her fingers stop moving. "All the time. Usually in the car. I'll look into the empty passenger seat like I used to when he was younger, and I wish he'd never grown up."

"Does it make you mad he didn't come for winter?"

"No."

I sniff.

She continues. "I'm happy that he's making his own way in life. Trying new things. Learning more about himself and what he wants. I'm proud of him, even though it hurts to feel the ties between us lengthen."

I shift my arm and look up at her. Her blue eyes are framed by dark hair like his. Hers is still short, not fully grown out yet like it was before she got sick. "Sorry," I murmur.

"What for?"

I shrug. "For being mad at him."

She leans down and kisses my forehead. "It's okay to feel that way. You'll be all right. We'll stick it out together. Before we know it, he'll be home for Christmas."

* * *

Come Christmas holidays, Annie, Darren, Bert, Ernie, and I are in Auckland to see Fat Freddy's Drop. I can barely concentrate on enjoying the music, knowing Jace is arriving in Wellington. I jump to the beat, banging into Darren and Ernie on either side of me. When it's half over, I sneak into the bathroom and call Dad's landline. Lila answers. "Yes, he's arrived!"

"All safe?"

"Yes, safe. A friend of his is staying for a couple of nights too. I've set up Annie's old room for him. She'll be staying in her flat when you guys get home, right?"

"Yeah." It sucks to have missed Jace's arrival but maybe it's for the best. Maybe it'll show him that his lack of contact hasn't hurt me at all.

Not at all.

Someone bangs on the door of my stall and tells me to hurry up. I flip him the bird as I wrap up the conversation and head back to the dance floor. The music scorches the air and makes me forget about reality for a few hours.

Afterwards, we take a bus to the beach close to our hotel. The sky is navy, streaked with purple rivulets, the last goodbye of today's sun. The cool sand is a pleasant contrast to the humid air, and the crashing waves mesmerize me with their glowing white tips. Annie and Darren are comparing thoughts about the concert—he liked it more than she did. He's trying to convince her she really loved it, and Annie is laughing against his chest. I smile and veer off to the water.

I've just taken my shoes off when Ernie bounds over. Bert is sitting on a piece of driftwood doing something on his phone.

"So," he says.

"So."

He shrugs and gets to it. "You've been distant this year."

No point in lying about it now. "A bit, yeah."

"We've been worried."

"I'm good. I'll be fine."

"Good. Sweet." He takes off his shoes and wades into the water with me. "We hope that you're going to be okay next year without us to keep you in check."

I laugh. "Yeah, thanks for keeping it real."

We stop walking, and our feet sink into the sand as the tide pulls out. "You've made me a better person, Coop. I never would have lifted a finger or done anything at school without your help. I might have laughed it off but it was really cool of you, man. Bert will never say it, but he loved that you watched his games even though rugby isn't your thing. You're solid, dude."

I don't know what to say. "You were both there for me too."

Another wave pulls the sand under our feet.

"I'm about sapped out." Ernie jerks a thumb toward the others. "Shall we?"

He moves to leave, and I snatch him back into a hug. The

next wave catches us at the backs of our knees, soaking the pants we'd rolled up. We thump each other between the shoulder blades three times and break apart.

lapis lazuli

As soon as our plane lands in Wellington, I beeline to the hatchback in long-term parking. Darren is dropping Annie off, and I'm stuck with Bert and Ernie, who are racing to keep up with me.

"Dude, what's the rush?"

"Nothing. Just want to get home."

Ernie slaps my shoulder. "You're kidding, right?" Ernie says this lightly, but he's been quieter today, sort of mellow, and I know he's thinking of Bert going to Auckland and me to Dunedin, leaving him here. "You can't leave us. We have a whole evening of drinking and debauchery planned."

"While that sounds positively awesome," I say, moving the seat forward to let Ernie in, "I'm going to pass."

"But—"

"I'll make it up to you."

Bert grumbles, shrugs.

"Promise."

That gets a small grin. "Next time we get together, it'd better be epic. Something to remember."

I drop them both at Ernie's and beat every traffic light home under the red evening sun. The inside of the house is illuminated but Dad and Lila's car isn't in the garage. I pull in, too excited to bother searching for a parking spot.

Okay, this is it. Nonchalance does it.

I run a hand through my hair and flatten my Radio One T-shirt. In my jean's pocket is a smooth, bottle-brown stone I found at Auckland harbor that morning.

I'm ready. At least, I will be ready as soon as my heart stops bashing my ribs.

What will Jace look like? Will he have filled out more? Will his hair be short, messy, untamed? Will he smile when he sees me? Will he forget everyone else?

Deep breath. One step at a time.

I race inside, throwing my keys onto the shelf by the garage door.

Jace could be out, I suppose. Out for dinner and forgot to switch off—

A creak from upstairs.

Jace!

I don't care that it's been weird between us for six long months. I'm going to crush him into a hug because dammit, I have missed him.

I take the steps two at a time and walk slowly down the hall. It won't look good to surprise him while puffing. The nerves! I pause for a moment to take a deep breath.

The hallway drags forever. Another creak beckons me to Jace's room. I pass the gaming room and the broom closet, trailing my fingers over the wall.

Dickweed, I'll tell him, *you should have called.*

And then I'll launch into the hug.

His bedroom door is closed, so I squeeze the cool handle as though it's one of my rocks. It instantly cuts through a blurred year, and unexpectedly, everything appears brighter, harder, colder. Even the air tastes sweeter.

I slowly push open the door—

Jace is sitting on the end of his bed, chin lifted, lips parted, his profile glowing amber in the evening sun. His T-shirt is bunched in one hand, and he's fumbling with the greenstone hook at his chest with the other.

I smile, fully prepared to race in and tackle him down to the—

He's not alone.

A mop of blond hair swirls vigorously in his lap.

The blur rushes back over me like thick fog. I wish it were thicker.

The guy with the mop of blond is on his knees sucking forcefully at Jace's cock. The bed creaks as Jace flexes deeper into his mouth. He lets the T-shirt go and threads his fingers around the guy's hair, then manually guides the depth and pace of his thrusts. The sucking and slurping is so fucking loud. How did I not hear it? How do they not fucking see me rooted in the doorway?

Jace moans and shuts his eyes. Blond Mop works faster, faster, faster—

Jace pushes the guy off him and comes in his hand.

I find the strength in my legs to silently shuffle backward to my room. The open door will be Jace's only clue.

I shut my door quietly behind me. I pull out the beach stone from Auckland. Just a regular stone. One of a million. I should never have gone into his room with just this. I should have had a piece of lapis lazuli—rich blue, the color of his eyes. A stone said to offer protection; a stone believed to foretell love that would be forever faithful.

With that in my pocket, I would have gone into Jace's room and left satisfied.

I speed-dial Ernie.

"About that debauchery—I've changed my mind. I'm in."

* * *

Bert and Ernie down a third shot of Tequila. I'm only on my second, but I'm halfway drunk already. The music rings obnoxiously in my ears and makes it impossible to think. I love it.

I don't want to think. I want to—

I throw back my shot, hop off the barstool, and sink into the crowd. The sweaty air smells of beer and citrus, threatening the nice buzz I have. *It's the wrong kind of citrus. Too sour.*

Dance!

The night becomes a blur of color, smiles, and whispers that coax me closer to some guy who is eye-fucking me from across the room. I saunter up and sway against him. His hands fumble under my shirt and over my back. He presses me against his stiff cock.

I shut my eyes against the image of Jace, head thrown back, moaning—

I slide my hand into my pocket and remove the stone. I drop it onto the dance floor and rub myself harder against my dance partner, who doesn't smell or feel like Jace, which is what I need. *Make me forget.* "What's your name?"

"Daniel." Doesn't sound like Jace, either. "Yours?"

I kick the stone as far away from us as possible. "Cooper."

marble

I wake at midday to the distant sound of yelling and laughing. My head pounds and my mouth is dry, tongue glued to the roof. I throw on a T-shirt and shorts before I hunt in the kitchen for water and a magic cure for hangovers.

I drink three glasses of water and take a pain killer.

Why do people think alcohol is fun?

Never again.

I rub my tender temples, moaning under my breath. My head feels like I've been bashing it against the marble counter.

I'm not proud. No matter how much I wanted to cut through the fog, going back to Daniel's place had been a mistake.

But at least I'm not a virgin anymore.

Flashes of my cock pushing into his ass while he moaned and begged make me blush again. I fling open the cupboard—*any* cupboard that will shield me from Lila.

Can't shield you from what happened, though.

Dizziness and shame war for dominance. I pull out a fresh cup and turn to the sink. Movement flutters outside the windows. Over the tier curtains, I observe Dad, Jace, and Blond Mop kicking around a soccer ball.

Lila slithers up to my side with the water jug and fills my cup with water.

"Jace missed you last night."

Somehow I doubt that.

"We came home with enough takeout to feed an army. Annie texted Dad and said you were on your way home and that she was going back to her flat. Said she'll come by tonight."

I finally draw away from the view of Dad juggling the ball and Jace copying him. "Bert and Ernie wanted us to hang."

The tea kettle whistles. I grab Annie's stash of green tea and force a spoonful into filter bags.

I feel justified and dirty at the same time.

Dirty.

I shiver. Despite showering for an hour, the bad memory from last night lingers.

Turn around. So I don't have to see your face. So I can imagine you're him.

I switch off the tea kettle and pour water over the tea leaves. We sit at the dining table, sipping.

It doesn't cleanse me as I hoped it would.

The back door bursts open and Dad strolls into the kitchen. "Cooper!" he says. "Brilliant, you can even up the teams. Get your shoes on."

"Nah, I don't feel like playing."

"Just half an hour. It'll be fun. You and your dad against Jace and Samuel."

Samuel.

I stare at a leaf floating in the last dregs of tea.

Dad will announce that I'm back home. I will have to face Jace and Samuel eventually—and rather than let Jace wonder why I refuse to come out now and say hello, I could have the upper hand. I could go out there and pretend like nothing matters. Like Jace and his friend are the last things on my mind.

All—thrust—*I*—thrust—*Want*—thrust—*Is*—thrust—*You, Jace.*

Jace? Who's Jace?

Heat floods every pore and I drink the last of my tea, leaf and all. "Okay." I pad toward the back door and slip on a pair of sneakers. They feel strange over bare feet but at this point, what doesn't?

I push through the back door and brusquely walk to Jace, who is standing with his back to me. Samuel sees me first but before Jace can turn, I throw an arm around him and thump his chest, right where the hook is. "Hey stranger," I say into his ear.

His body tenses for a moment, and his muscles shift as he twists around and grabs me into a bear hug. He holds me so tightly I can barely breathe, but my insides twist and tears prick at my eyes. True to form, he smells faintly like oranges.

"Cooper," he says against my neck. His words ooze hurt and regret, surprise and joy. The way he clutches me says everything. *I'm sorry I didn't call you. I just didn't know how to tell you I met someone else. I didn't know how to say I've moved on. But I've missed you, I have. You're my friend. My brother.*

I break away from the hug, struggling to hold myself together. I summon every ounce of willpower to extend a hand to Samuel.

He's shorter than Jace and I, and I'm happy about this. "Samuel," he says. "Jace's . . . friend." Samuel's gaze flashes nervously to Jace's, and I follow it.

Jace swallows. He knows I'm staring at him but he won't look over.

Dad kicks the soccer ball into our midst and joins us. "Cooper and I against you Otago boys."

We play, and despite the hangover, I kick and weave and score in earnest. No one can stop me because I can't let them. Won't let them.

After twenty minutes, Dad calls for a break. I juggle the ball in the corner of the field as I let them catch their breath. Jace moves close to Samuel and says something in his ear while rubbing his upper arm. He breaks away and jogs over to me.

I keep juggling. Three, four, five, six—header—seven, eight—

"I know what you're thinking, but don't do it, okay?" Jace whispers.

I catch the ball and hold it under my arm. "Don't do what?" My glare drifts over to Samuel, who's making my dad laugh.

Jace steps closer, chuckling and shaking his head. "I see it on your face. The way you look at him." He pries the ball from me. "You want to kick this ball in his face just like you did to me."

"I saw you two," I say.

He stills and mutters, "The door. That was you then?"

"Do you love him?"

A sigh. "He's my boyfriend."

Boyfriend. Boyfriend. Boyfriend. "Told the folks you're gay yet?"

"Bisexual, and yes, that kind of came up last night."

I don't bother to ask if they took it well. Of course they did.

Boyfriend.

"How long?"

"Since before winter but we were mates for a bit first."

"How did you meet?"

He quiets, then says, "Kepler Track. A mate invited him along on our hike."

I'm shaking as I recall his words: *This stone made sleeping impossible. It kept digging into my back, so I snuck out of the tent in the middle of the night, lifted the pegs, and pulled it out. Still couldn't sleep, though. After that, all I could think about was* rocks.

Was it really the stone that interrupted his sleep?

"Kepler Track," I repeat. I walk backward, blindly moving toward the house.

"Just a second," Jace calls out to Dad and Samuel as he chases after me.

I run up the stairs before he can stop me, but I'm not fast enough to slam the door in his face.

He pushes in and I ignore him, fishing for my damn phone.

I scroll through my contacts until I find last night's mistake. On the third ring, "Daniel here."

"Hey, Daniel, Cooper here. Wanted to see how you're doing."

He murmurs. "Good. Real good."

"Last night was—good for me too. We should do it again

some time."

"Sounds goo—"

Jace smacks the phone out of my hand. It hits the floor so hard the screen cracks. Before I can chase after the call, Jace spins me around. His jaw is clenched and his gaze is livid.

"What are you doing?"

"Same thing you are."

"Not the same thing. I *know* Samuel."

Samuel, not Sam? "You've no idea how well I know Daniel—"

"You should've held out until you found someone you care about!"

"You care about Samuel?"

I realize I've been clinging to the hope that their relationship is only about sex. But he actually *cares*?

I turn so he doesn't see the traitorous tear running down my cheek.

"Well, I mean, yeah, he's a good guy."

I nod and pick up my phone, which mirrors my cracked reflection. Fitting.

"I'm sorry I didn't tell you," he continues as I slouch on the side of my bed. "But I had to make those feelings go away." *You want to have normal ones, not about your maybe brother.*

"I don't care," I say.

Jace rocks on his heels. Hesitates. Whispers, "I do."

I opt to stay in Wellington after all, accepting a position at Vic. Part of the way through the second year of my undergraduate studies, Jace performs as pianist in a ballet accompaniment. Dad and Lila fly to the opening show, and though I'm not invited, I take the hatchback over on the ferry and drive down to Dunedin.

I don't announce my presence.

All the affordable tickets are sold out, so I fork out a chunk of my savings for a seat far too close to where Jace is playing.

I slip on sunglasses and sink into my seat until the lights dim and the ballet begins. I focus on the music and Jace with his back to me, his fingers dancing over the keys and mesmerizing me. Dressed in a suit with tails, he takes me back to Newtown High and the dance we shared. Only now Jace fills his suit better, and he's grown into a man.

What wouldn't I give to dance with *this* man?

First, though, we'd need to be on speaking terms. At least, more than the generic fluff. *Merry Christmas. Happy New Year. Is Mum around? Tell Dad happy birthday. Happy New Year. Happy twentieth, Jace.*

Happy nineteenth, Cooper.

No, there'll be no dancing anytime soon.

Still, this is his biggest recital. I wouldn't miss it for all the money in the world.

During intermission, his face splits into a grin when he spots his parents. Behind my shades, I follow his gaze. Lila, Dad, and a young woman in a sleek navy dress with raven hair to match. She smiles a seductive smile back at Jace, as though she's promising to do secretive things to him when the curtain closes.

In my mind, I hear Jace over Skype telling Lila and Dad about her. *Natalie's a singer, her voice is . . . impossible. She's beautiful, I hope for you to meet her.*

She's my opposite in every way: female, petite, dark features, and a talent for music I will never have.

My spirits sink, but I'm well-accustomed to being hurt by Jace's boyfriends and girlfriends.

The lights dim and the ballet begins again. The music soothes the remnants of my old heartaches. The only thing I can do is smile and clap bloody hard for how beautifully Jace played.

I slink out of the audience before anyone spots me.

At the crack of dawn the next morning, I begin the drive back home, stopping at the Moeraki Boulders. The seaweed-tasting air has a cool bite as it whips sand against the beach's boulders. A few tourists take pictures of the fifty-six-million-year-old rocks, but I head over to lean against a smaller boulder.

The cool rock hums over my skin like it's sharing its memories.

I've borne witness to pain. I've seen canoes tip and people drown. I've collected the tears of a thousand men who have leaned against me and cried like you do. I've borne witness to joy—celebrations and laughter that echoed off me and settled onto my boulder brothers. Laughs that still vibrate under the surface.

I've existed since before myth and legend, long enough to become one. Did you know the Maori believed us to be remains of their eel baskets and sweet potatoes that washed ashore during the wreck of a large sailing canoe?

I'm a rock. The closest thing to eternal.

An anthology of stories that never end.

I smile and trace my name over its surface. Then his.

The tide sweeps in around us as if to soak up my story and run away. I envision it out there being tossed up onto the rocky surface.

Has our story ended? If so, will it sink to the bottom of the ocean, near the aquamarines that mermaids treasure? Or will heavy breezes whip it through the sky, carrying it over every surface because it's not finished yet?

An eerie shiver follows me as I make my way back to the hatchback and continue my way to Wellington.

In a rural, coastal stretch between Christchurch and Picton, the hatchback splutters and dies. I view this annoying incident as my answer—confirmation my story has sunk.

I call roadside help, and they tow the dead car to Kaikoura, a small town.

Long story short, she's not worth starting again.

I say my goodbyes and start trekking down the main road, thumb out, looking for a ride. Five cars pass before one slows down and flashes its lights at me. I jog over pebbles—pick a small one up—and slide into the silver car.

The driver is wearing board shorts and a Flight of the Conchords T-shirt. His crooked smile reveals a slight gap between his front teeth. Five or so years older than me, I'd guess.

His brown eyes are warm but slightly nervous.

I shake his hand. "Cooper. My car died, and I'd love to get up toward Picton."

He grins. "Zach. And it just so happens I'm taking the ferry there to Wellington."

Christmas, and Zach and I have been dating for months now. I want to surprise Annie with a beautiful kauri rocking chair I found at a warehouse out in Petone. It cost a fortune, but since Annie was moving into a single apartment and had just landed a job as a school counselor, I really wanted to get her something special.

Zach drives me and the chair, strapped into the trunk, to Annie's new apartment on Christmas morning. He yawns and shakes his head. "Why so early?"

"Because she woke me at six on my birthday. It's time for payback."

Zach mumbles something about getting me back for getting *him* up so early, and I promise I'll make it up to him later. He perks up and grins.

I laugh, leaning over to kiss his stubbly cheek. "Merry Christmas, Zach."

As soon as we arrive at Annie's, Zach parks the car, races around to my side and pulls me out. He nips my lips and kisses me against the car door. "You taste like peppermint," he says as I pull a half-eaten candy cane out of my pocket.

He laughs and pilfers it. The beast.

We carry the chair up the steep incline to the small, one-bedroom house overlooking the bush and a wedge of ocean. I leave the chair at the front door with Zach and sneak off around the house to Annie's bedroom.

Her window is partially open, and I'm about to cry out Merry Christmas and swing inside when I hear a guy laugh and say, "Here. This is for you. Merry Christmas."

I freeze. I recognize his voice.

"You didn't have to," Annie says. A long beat, then—

"Do you like them?"

"I love them. I love *you*—"

We gasp at the same time. Footsteps stomp across the floorboards and the curtains are flung open. I am face to face with Ernie.

His face pales but he keeps his head high. Annie pushes open the window and glares at me. A long pair of emerald earrings glimmer in the morning light, making her eyes brighter.

"I came to surprise you," I say slowly. "Turns out you beat me to it again, Annie. What's going on?"

My attention narrows to Ernie and the thin pair of boxers he's wearing.

"I'm in love with her. I'm in love with Annie."

Annie blushes and smiles coyly at their feet before leaning over and kissing his cheek just the way I did with Zach.

Ernie brushes her hair over her shoulders. "Maybe it's time to tell your brother?"

She laughs and gestures to me. "Come to the front, we'll let you in."

Ernie has changed into a pair of jeans and a tank top when he and Annie open the door and let me, Zach, and the chair inside the dining room.

Annie coos over the chair until I start tapping my foot. Zach comes up behind me, wraps his arms around my waist and tells me to take a breath. Love is a wonderful feeling.

I relax against him, but I wonder if Zach is growing impatient with my excuses not to say *I love you.*

I block out the worry and concentrate instead on Ernie, who is nervously preparing some tea.

"How long?" I ask.

Annie answers, "A year."

A whole year? My closest friend and my sister?

"Longer, Annie," Ernie says. "And you know it."

She rocks in her new chair. "It grew slowly, I don't know how long it's been going on but it's a year since we—"

"I don't need to know all the details."

Ernie laughs. "Fine. I've been smitten with your sister from the first time I saw her."

Smitten? The word sounds foreign coming from Ernie's mouth. "You didn't say anything."

"Dude. She's your sister. Be weird if I told you how much she turns me on and that every day I wank—"

And *there*'s the Ernie I know. "I pray to God you don't finish that sentence."

Annie stifles a giggle.

"I get it. You didn't tell me you had a crush on her." I shake my head at Annie. "How on earth did you fall for this guy?"

I love Ernie, I do, but there's a degree of stupid that people shouldn't overlook.

Annie stops rocking. "Actions speak louder than words. Ernie shows me every day how much he cares. It started when he danced with you at Newtown High."

"You fell for him all the way back then? I thought you liked Darren?"

"I did like Darren back then."

"Good things take time," Ernie says, handing me a cup of tea. "I'm a good thing."

Annie grins. "Took me a while to figure it out."

"I hated when you hooked up with Darren," Ernie says, twisting a chair from the table and straddling it. "Bert and Cooper joined in my grief that day in the form of debauchery. Never been so drunk in my life."

How did I not recognize Ernie was suffering as much as I was that fateful day? I pull out a chair and slump onto it. "I'm sorry, Ernie. I didn't know."

"You had your own problems. We all did."

Zach stands behind me, rubbing my shoulders. I tilt my head back and smile at him. He leans down and kisses me. For a second, it's almost enough and I'm close to something like love for him. Maybe if I wait long enough, it will grow on me like it did with my sister and Ernie.

"Why didn't you tell me earlier?" I ask, lifting my tea and taking a sip. The liquid is warm but hasn't been boiled.

He makes her tea the way she likes it.

"Because—"

"Because I was afraid you would turn her away from me," Ernie says. "I say stupid things sometimes, and you know all the shit I've done. How could you take me seriously? How could you see past those parts to the real ones? I love Annie, and I'm scared one day she'll see how much more amazing she is than me. As selfish as it might've been, I didn't want you to give her a head start."

I take another sip of tea.

I stand and lean down to hug Annie. I breathe in the soapy scent of her hair, and I flinch at her cold earring against my cheek.

Emeralds. Ernie's birthstone. Ernie walks into view and I hold his nervous stare. "They say so long as the friendship is true, emeralds will stay in one piece. I hope yours never break, Annie."

She nods, chin banging against my shoulder. "They won't. I won't let them."

serpentinite

I bring Zach home to Mum's for my twentieth. This is the first time they've met, and Zach is taking it all in stride. Why have I waited so long to show him off?

He leans back in his chair, the brown of his T-shirt complementary against the dark wood. He fits at this table, fits in conversation with Mum and Paul, jokes casually with Ernie, and listens carefully to Annie. He *fits* here, and he should fit with me too.

I grab his hand under the table and rub my thumb in circles at his wrist.

Paul refills Mum's teacup. Their gazes catch, and with the orange sun streaming through the skylight, the scene glistens and shines like well-polished crystal.

"Zach," Mum says, smiling widely as she focuses on him, "you're a social worker?"

Zach squeezes me and gently pries his fingers free. He rests his arms on the table as he nods. Half of him is in a square of light that makes his arm hair glisten gold. "Yes, I basically take care of kids in bad situations."

"That sounds like a tough job."

I've seen Zach so emotionally drained from a day's work that he doesn't have enough energy to do anything but sleep. He's strong, though. Persevering through the hard shit and the threats he gets on a weekly basis. *For the kids*, he says.

Zach takes a sip of tea. "It's tough, and sometimes it feels useless. I like that we run family conferences and care and protection meetings, but sometimes it's not enough. Then we have to move the kids."

"Difficult. Do you keep in contact with the kids you help once they're placed in care?"

"For a while, to make sure everything is running smoothly. But eventually I move on. Though I make sure the kids always know they can call me."

Zach's arms have broken out in goosebumps, reminding me of last week when Zach brought up one of his toughest cases. His first. We were in my flat, alone, thanks to my flatmates skipping off to the Waiarapa for the weekend. After making us dinner, I found him leaning forward on the couch, elbows on his knees as he scrubbed his face.

"You okay?"

"Yeah." He stares at his phone on the coffee table. "Just got a message from someone I helped out a couple of years ago."

"A kid? Are they okay?"

He shrugs. "I have no idea. It didn't say much. Might have been sent accidentally."

"Do you have to call and check?"

"No, he's nineteen. He'll make his own way in the world."

I set the dinner on the coffee table. "You helped him when he was seventeen? I thought—"

"Yes, no, I helped his younger brother. Hamish took his brother away from their abusive parents to protect him, but things got bad when their parents discovered them."

"Shit. I'm sorry."

Zach's laugh startles me back to my birthday breakfast, and I blink at the untouched pancakes on my plate.

"I love to surf," Zach says. "It's a great way of purging tension." He kisses my cheek. "I'm going to teach this one a few tricks this summer."

Annie leans over to Ernie. "You should get lessons too."

The doorbell rings.

After a few moments, Mum comes back. "Cooper, a visitor for you."

I push back my chair and wander toward the front door. Standing at the threshold, morning light framed behind him, is Jace. He has his hands shoved into his pockets, and he's turned away from the house, staring out at the wild garden as he waits.

I breathe in a nectar-scented breeze. "Jace?" I say quietly.

He turns slowly. His gaze is guarded but as he takes me in, a slow grin warms his face. His eyes glitter brightly—the first I've seen since forever ago.

"Cooper," he says softly.

"What are you doing here?" The wooden floorboards cool the soles of my feet, helping to ground me.

He stammers and has to take a deep breath. He tries again. "Happy birthday, Jace. Happy birthday, Cooper. Merry Christmas—when did that happen? After our one-minute call on my birthday, I couldn't stop thinking about how we used to talk for hours. I want—I wish—"

Footsteps bang down the hall, followed by voices—my sister and Zach. She's telling him about some embarrassing photos of me that he'll love.

"Oh, wait. Jace?" Annie's steps approach faster, and Zach is nearing too. "Hey, I didn't know you were coming home." Wellington, she means.

"Just for the weekend," Jace says, glancing curiously at the other man coming up behind me. "I had something I wanted to do." His gaze lands on mine, and he pulls something from his pocket.

I take it and smile. A gift. It's small, hard and heavy.

Jace smiles too. "Happy—"

Zach wraps his arm around my neck, sliding close to me, and extends his other hand. "You're the brother, right?"

I wince.

It's subtle but Jace reels back. His now-stiff smile solidifies on his face, as if it's taking everything in his power to keep it there.

"Yes, his brother." Reluctantly, he takes the offered hand.

Jace swallows and looks away. "Well, I wanted to wish you a happy birthday. Dad wants to know what you want for your birthday dinner." He shrugs, already moving across the veranda. "Call him. I gotta go. My girlfriend is waiting in the car."

He gives us a short wave. "Later."

* * *

Except Jace is not at Dad's later. He's gone, his room void of anything to prove he was even here.

Lila seems saddened by his abrupt departure.

"Maybe he and his girlfriend wanted alone time?"

She frowns. "What girlfriend?"

* * *

Zach and I go back to his place for the night. Still stuffed from dinner, we lounge on his comfy grey couch. A documentary about milk production plays on the television, but we're not paying much attention. We lie lengthwise on his couch, cuddling and nibbling little kisses on each other's neck.

His phone buzzes against my crotch, and I laugh.

"Sorry." He sits up and pulls out his phone, then pauses when he sees the sender. He frowns, and after a second, lies the phone down.

"Who is it?"

He swallows. "Hamish."

"The big brother you helped?"

He nods, but instead of curling up next to me again, he sits upright.

"Who is Hamish?"

"You just said—"

"No, I mean, who is he to you?"

"Just . . . someone."

Emotions flicker over his face, and I get it. “Someone special though, right?”

A long moment. “Yeah. But that was in the past.”

I brush my shoulder against his. “It’s okay, Zach. I have a past as well.”

He glances at me. “Do you want to talk about it?”

“I don’t think I can.”

“Yeah. I get it. Neither can I.” He twists and kisses me.

I brush his hair back and rub my nose against his.

“You’re beautiful,” he says simply. “You have no idea how happy I am I pulled over that day.”

“Me too.”

argillite

Argillite. The basement-of-New-Zealand rock.

Deformed. Fractured. Veined. Argillite has endured 300 million years of tectonic movement. And Zach and I are driving over it on our way to Auckland for a concert.

Our first stop was New Plymouth to visit Zach's cousin, and now we're on the road again, driving up the coast with the windows wide open. Salty sea air slowly turns earthy—the smell of a thousand sheep.

I change gears and wind around a blind corner. More rolling green hills spotted with sheared sheep. The sun beams brightly through the windshield, and Zach and I simultaneously pull down our sun visors.

Zach pulls out my sunglasses from the glove compartment and hands them to me. He doesn't say anything. In fact, the whole trip so far, he's been fidgeting and squirming.

I flash him a smile to calm him, even though my insides are tight. Does he want to tell me something? Does he think we'd be better off friends? The thought makes me cold because I care about Zach. He's funny, he's sweet, and he's great in bed.

Zach shifts in his seat, picking at his seat belt like it's constricting him of air. "Cooper," he whispers much too softly for my comfort.

A shiver rolls over me, making my heart race and my stomach churn. What if he wants more? What if he wants to talk about the future?

Zach clogs up again, grumbles and turns on the radio to classic rock. Cat Steven's *The First Cut is the Deepest* plays. The lyrics gently wrap around me until I'm living the song. The song is me. The song is us. I want Zach by my side.

Even though I don't know if I can love again.

I push my sunglasses higher up on my nose so Zach won't try to read me. The next half-hour, I am lost in thoughts. I don't even hear the other songs play. I focus on the road and the way the breeze rolls over grass, making the hills shimmer and feel alive, like a green beast who will stretch his limbs and sit up at any moment.

And maybe we'd drive down his arm to his large fist, where he'd crush us to dust with all the memories I can't seem to shake.

Like the time Jace and I took the hatchback out to Kaitoke Regional Park to see Rivendell, and Jace had breathed deeply and said *It really feels like there's magic here. I wouldn't be surprised if the trees actually came to life—*

I slow down and glance at Zach's large hands, slightly bumpy with veins. I squeeze his fingers.

I care. I care. I care.

Don't leave me.

Don't ask me to stay.

He plays with my fingers for a moment before I pull away to steer around another stretch of winding road.

We're in the middle of a curve when the song comes on.

"Turn it off," I plead.

Zach sounds surprised. "What? This is a great song."

In my mind's eye, I see Jace's smile as he says *diamonds*.

I breathe in sharply. "Turn it off!"

He does, and the silence is loaded with questions that I don't want to answer. "I'm just dizzy," I say, curving around another bend. "The music is too much."

Zach frowns, apparently not buying it, but he lets it go and asks me to pull over.

I do.

He leans over and kisses me deeply, and then pops open my seatbelt. "How about I drive for a bit?"

We swap places, and I lean back against the seat wondering where he is now. Wondering what his life is like. Whether he finds it hard to fall in love again too. I shut my eyes and let the vibrations of the car take me to a dreamy world of giants and rocks and unanswered questions.

* * *

I wake to Zach shaking me gently. "Thought we'd take a stop. I saw a sign for this place and knew we had to come here."

I take off my sunglasses and rub the bridge of my nose where they pressed awkwardly. I blink in the brightness of the day.

Zach is saying how he always wanted a chance to go here, and when he saw the sign, he knew it was meant to be.

I stretch, ripping out a yawn, and Zach tickles my midriff. I laugh on instinct and yank my T-shirt down.

"Where are—"

Waitomo Caves. The universe just slapped me in the face.

Zach grabs our jackets. "Mr. Geologist, are you ready?"

No.

I follow him anyway. Forty minutes later, we are inching along a narrow passage down a limestone shaft. Our guide talks about the formations but I can barely focus with the shivers running through me.

Our song, and now this? Are these signs?

How many earthquakes can our relationship withstand? Are we as strong as argillite?

I clutch my phone in my pocket, yearning to call Jace.

Zach looks over his shoulder and smiles. With every smile, guilt worms itself deeper into my belly.

If you can't love him completely, set him free. He deserves better.

But I care! I really do!

We hop on a boat. It's cool and dark with a distant sound of dripping. Zach takes my hand as we glide into the Glowworm Grotto.

I gasp. It's like we're floating in space with galaxies at our fingertips. The darkness thickens and pushes me from behind toward the edge of a high cliff. The rush is unbearable as it comes coupled with memories.

As kids in the cave.

All I Want Is You.

Zach whispers in my ear, and my stomach flips. Now I know what he's going to ask me, and I'm not ready for it. Certainly not when Jace's ghost is here dancing with me.

Don't. Don't. Don't.

"Will you move in with me?"

muscovite

Jace's twenty-second birthday.

My sister, Lila, and Dad huddle around the laptop in Dad's study, Skyping him as we do every year. I slunk out after a tense *Happy Birthday, Jace*. He frowned but waved me goodbye.

Lila and Dad speak to him for a few more minutes, asking him how he's doing. I know this, because I'm standing just outside the study in the shadows.

Part of me doesn't want to stay here, forcing out fake conversation; another part wants nothing more than to hear his voice, forever, on repeat, even if he said nothing more than a shopping list.

"We have news," Dad says. I hold my breath, knowing what's coming because I helped dad pick out a diamond ring and gold bands. "We wanted to wait to tell you in person, but—"

"We can't wait," Lila chirps in. She gestures Dad to spit it out already. He laughs, smacks her with a kiss, and says, "Your mum and I are getting married."

"Wow, oh my God, congratulations!" Jace's tone is enthusiastic. "About time, I guess."

Lila says, "We've also decided on a date."

Annie says, "You better come, brother. No ditching us like you always seem to do."

Jace says, "Of course I'm going to the wedding! I've never ditched you."

Even Lila and Dad quiet at that. Lila speaks first. "Never mind that. I would love you to walk me down the aisle—"

"Yes. When is it?"

Annie snickers. "Three guesses."

Jace got it right on the second. "Dad's birthday? You're kidding."

Dad and Annie chuckle. "Dad wants *everything* on his day. Wait until you hear the theme they have."

Jace says, "Mum? You agreed to this? A Halloween-birthday-masquerade wedding with a dress code of hauntingly beautiful?"

Lila laughs. "Sounds like fun to me."

The doorbell rings. Guests Lila and Dad invited over to share the big news. Lila air-kisses Jace and excuses herself. Dad says they'll call again soon.

They're kissing as they leave the room and don't notice me hunkered outside the doorway. I rest my head against the wall and shut my eyes to all this romance. I'm happy for Lila and Dad, but I'm still raw from last week—

Jace says, "So . . . sister, eh?"

"Yep, been a long while coming."

"Guess so." A moment of silence, and then, "Cooper didn't say much. I mean, I guess that's normal. But he usually stays. Listens."

I close my eyes.

Annie hums. "Just ignore Cooper, Jace. He's moping around because he broke up with his boyfriend."

Quiet. A crackle down the line. "He did?"

Annie sighs on my behalf. "Yeah."

My heart beats heavy in my chest three, four times before he replies. "Oh," I wish to hear an edge of satisfaction, a splash of glee that gives away how relieved he is to hear this. But his tone is merely genuine. "I hope he'll be okay."

Annie gives a slight laugh. "Yeah. Besides, we're used to it."

I hold my breath and pray for Annie to leave it at that.

Jace asks, "Used to it?"

"Yeah. He was worse when you left."

gold

Dad and Lila tie the knot, exchanging beautiful gold bands. The wedding is just what they wish for. Hauntingly beautiful.

For the wedding reception, the doors to the patio open to eight round tables, each peppered with twelve guests.

I sip on my ginger beer, cucumber, and gin cocktail, and take in the colorful festivity, which is like a sea of melted crayons—women wear large skirts and corsets, and men wear tailored suits fit with vests. Like something from Cinderella's ball but with grotesque twists: dripping blood, ripped bodices, deadly-long nails, red contact lenses, and fake scars.

Lila and Dad sit at the head of our table, an arch framing them from behind. The spider webs that cover the arch are made with hundreds of stringed faux-beryl crystals that sparkle under the fairy lights behind them.

Lila and Dad both wear white—Dad, a suit with a dried silver rose drooping out of his pocket. Lila, a gown with the same dead silver roses woven in the bodice. They feed each other olive-pesto-stuffed capsicums, and nibble kisses on each other's fingers.

A hand lands on my shoulder, jerking me out of my observations.

"What're you daydreaming about, pussycat?" Ernie asks, shifting his chair a touch nearer. Dressed in a black suit with white buttons, a bow tie, and a bowler hat, Ernie has a cross of wood hanging with string slung over his back. He'd held it above Annie as they arrived. Puppet and Puppeteer.

He waves a hand in front of my face. "Calling Cooper . . ."

I slap him away with a chuckle. "It's all so much but I'm happy for them."

Ernie drinks his cocktail and stares at Dad and Lila. "You've got an awesome family, Cooper."

He focuses his gaze on me and grins, but it's a shy grin; one I'm not used to seeing on him. "I hope one day I can be a part of it."

I sit straighter, my foot knocking into the leg of the table. "You and Annie?"

I don't say the rest, but he bites his lip and nods.

"I never thought I could ever be so lucky. She's special."

"Yes, she is."

"Would you bless it, if I—"

"You're going to ask?"

"Soon."

I pull him into a hug. "If you hurt my sis, I'll make your life miserable."

"Good. If I did that, I'd deserve it."

Annie comes and whispers something to Ernie. He nods and she leaves.

"What's that about?"

"She's got a little something to do."

The waiters serve parmesan-lemon risotto with fried oyster mushrooms and roasted cauliflower purée.

Jace's chair is hauntingly vacant. He flew in a few days ago but other than stiff hellos and awkward conversation, we've avoided each other.

As though we wanted to say more but didn't know how, we ducked into bathrooms or the kitchen pantry or the garage when we caught sight of the other. I'd seen him enough to know he looked the same, with a few more creases around the eyes. Laughter I hadn't been part of.

I search the crowd for his Prince Charming suit: a gold blazer with brass buttons, tassels coming off the shoulders, and a blue sash. I don't see—

The music and chattering crowds hush to a silence.

Jace's voice comes over the speakers, laughter at the edges. "For Mum and Dad, may this day haunt you and your dreams forever."

The first few strokes of the piano echo in my belly. It's perfect in every way.

"*Time Warp*!" Lila cries. She starts singing along with Jace, while Dad pitches his voice higher and Annie's voice hits the speakers.

Ernie grins at my sideways stare. His huge grin lights up the room more than fairy light wetas dangling from the ceilings as chandeliers. "She's great, right?"

"Yeah, yeah." The food is delicious, but all I can do is stare and pick at it.

"You all right?" Ernie asks, eying my food like he wants to gobble my plate.

I slide it over to him. "Fine. I need the bathroom anyway."

I zigzag through the crowds to the arch leading to the foyer and the band. Jace has removed his blazer and plays with graceful energy. My sister and Jace are sharing a stool and a microphone. I lean in the shadows of the doorway and wish I knew a comfortable way to minimize the distance between us.

I slink back into the dining room crowds and make my way to the kitchen, which is temporarily repurposed into a bar. I perch on a stool and order whiskey. I sip and observe the head table outside. At the tail end of my drink, Annie and Jace return for their dinner.

I swirl the last sip of whiskey, ice clinking against the side of the glass. Rings of condensation mark the marble bench.

Someone tugs on my sleeve. I twist. Annie in a smooth doll mask. "Help me for a minute?"

"Sure."

She pinches my sleeve and drags me to the back room where the wedding gifts are stored. The whole side of one room is filled with colorfully wrapped boxes with large, obnoxious bows.

"What's up?" she asks, pulling her mask up to her pinned hair.

"Sorry? What do you—?"

"Mean? Don't think I haven't noticed how weird you two are acting. Ernie said you were acting weird too."

I swallow. "I don't know what you're talking about."

"That might work on someone else but not your sister. I know you. You haven't spoken to Jace all evening. Barely at all since he came home. What happened?"

I shift in my boots and brace a hand on my fake sword. The cape I'm wearing seems to be choking me and I unclasp it. The black material puddles at my feet. "It's been a busy few days, we just haven't had time—"

"Not the last three days. What happened to *you two*? You used to be best friends." She moves to the present pile and traces her fingers over the tops of bows and ribbons. "There was even a time when I thought—" She shakes her head. "Never mind."

The truth of her suspicions shows in the way she looks at me then looks away.

I fold my arms over a shiver. "What did you think?"

Annie stills her hand on the largest present, silver with drops of fake blood, the one I gave Dad and Lila. "I—I mean . . ."

Her inability to form the sentence confirms it. I sigh, glad for the whiskered mask even though it doesn't change facts.

"And if it was true?" I ask, voice cracking.

"I don't care." She lifts her chin and stares right at me. "Broken home, broken rules, right?"

My throat tightens and I shut my eyes for a few beats. Annie closes the distance between us and rubs my upper arm. "That type of broken is something we all have to live with and accept; but the broken between you and Jace . . . we all feel it. Dad and Lila too. We want things to be good between you."

God, how I wished that too.

Annie kisses my cheek under the mask. "Let's go back out. We could dance?"

But I don't think I can face a crowd yet. I need a moment to pull myself together. "Maybe later?"

"Right. I'd better check Dad isn't pulling Ernie apart piece by piece."

The air stirs as she shuts the door. I move to the window seat and sit.

Broken home, broken rules.

I breathe in the sharp relief of her words and peel off my mask. I peer at the darkness outside, the windowpane cold against my forehead. My breath fogs against the glass, and I scribble Jace's name through it. I wish things could be how they were then—

The door bursts open. I scrub Jace's name off the window and leap from the windowsill.

Dad and Lila stop kissing when they see me. "What are you doing in here?"

What are *you* doing in here? "Just making sure my gift was in order."

Lila giggles. "Your dad and I just wanted to . . . peek at the gifts."

Yeah, *that's* what they were doing in here. "Well don't let me stop you." I cut toward the door but Dad slings an arm across my neck. "This is the happiest day of my life. Thank you for making everything so wonderful."

In the distance, a loud scream sounds remarkably like Ernie.

Dad laughs. "And it just got better."

I grin. "How many other tricks do you have up your sleeve?"

Lila grabs a present and vigorously unwraps it. "You can also find treats upstairs."

I leave them to their shenanigans and head toward the chocolate-lava cake. Ernie's fake blood drips all down his front and he's swearing under his breath. "They're going to pay for that."

"Oh, yes," Annie says, dabbing his neck with a napkin. "Let me help you plot."

I sit and shift my chair in closer to the table. A piece of paper catches my eye. Slipped under my dessert plate is an envelope with my name on it. I pause before picking it up. No note. Just a smooth teal stone shaped like an hourglass.

I rub it between my fingers. "Did you leave—" I stop asking Annie and Ernie if they left the envelope here. I know who did.

I slip the stone into my pocket and search the room for him. For a while I think he left the reception, but then I spot him.

He looks different without his blazer, and he's wearing a mask made up of little silver squares that reflect the light like a disco ball. It's a different mask than the blue one he arrived in. Does he hope to lose himself in the crowd? Does he think I won't recognize his eyes, his mouth, his ears, his hands?

I left my mask in the gift room, but I'm not going back there so I pluck a paua shell one from the centerpiece and put it on before making my way to the bar.

I slip onto the stool next to him. Jace startles but doesn't acknowledge me. He sips his drink nonchalantly instead.

I order one of what he's having. "You here for the bride or the groom?"

Jace's hand jerks around his glass but otherwise he's still. He looks at me for a long moment. "Bride," he says. "We go way back."

"Groom," I say, leaning in conspiratorially. "Once I saw the guy swear at an old lady for cutting in line, and she whipped out her cane and tripped him in the parking lot. I'm Cooper, by the way, and who are you, Mr. Friend of the Bride?"

Jace laughs uncertainly. His gaze flashes to the bartender and the whiskey bottles. "Call me Wesley."

I lift my tumbler glass and drink deeply. The warm whiskey burns as it slides down my throat. I cough and chuckle at myself. "What do you think of the Halloween-birthday-masquerade wedding? I think the guy is after the gifts."

"Could be. Makes sense. He'll get twice as many. What did you get him?"

I grin. "See the biggest gift?"

"The one taking up the entire corner of the room?"

"Yep. That's mine."

"What is it?"

"Twenty cardboard boxes each smaller than the last."

"Ouch. What did he do to you?"

I shrug. "He's my dad. That's reason enough." I take another sip. "But there's a photo album of our family in the last box."

Jace rattles the ice in his glass. "Big family?"

"No, just broken."

"Sorry."

"Don't be. Broken family, broken rules. I had two birthdays, two Christmases, two great homes. I hope the album shows him how much I love him and Lila."

He blinks and parts his lips—

I cling my glass against his. "What is it you do, Wesley?"

He clears his throat. "I just finished university—teacher's college—but I plan on travelling around Europe for a year before I settle into a teaching career."

I hold back my surprise and draw my tumbler over the condensation on the bench. I knew Jace finished teacher's training but I didn't know he was planning to travel. "Wow." I take a much larger drink. "When does your adventure begin?"

"A few weeks. I wanted to be here for the wedding first."

I nod, trying to shake off the disappointment. A whole year away?

How is being in Europe different than in Dunedin if you never speak anyway? "Where will you go?"

"All over, really. I'll start with Germany and go from there."

"Sounds amazing. Make sure you go to Turkey to see the Göreme Fairy Chimneys. And the Giant's Causeway in Ireland, and of course, Stonehenge."

"Have you been?"

"No but one day I will. After I finish my masters."

"You really should."

"Teacher's college, what was that like?" *What has happened to you in the past years? What have I missed?*

"I taught one class where a kid got his hand stuck in a tuba. I don't know how he did it but it was jammed in there. We tried pulling, rotating, even using soapy water to dislodge him. I had to send him to First Aid. The class was in a shambles, and the only way I could pull in everyone's attention was to tell them about getting stuck up to my waist in mud while hiking a couple of years ago. It took me three hours with the help of some mates to get free."

I shake my head, grinning.

"What I didn't tell the class was that I lost my pants in the process and came out butt naked." Jace winces and takes another sip. "I'll never live it down."

"That's a good one."

"What about you?" he asks. "Any embarrassing stories?"

I shrug. What the hell. "My ex and I went bungee jumping at the Kawarau Bridge near Queenstown last year."

"Bungee jumping. You're crazy."

"When you're on the bridge, they ask if you want to touch the water. I didn't have a change of clothes with me so I said I'd like to touch it but not get dunked. They fiddled about with the ropes until it was my turn. I freaked out for a few moments then jumped. I crashed through the surface of the water and bounced back out. The rush was so intense that I didn't immediately notice something was off. But as the bounces slowed, I became aware of cold air on my butt and . . . that's when I noticed the water had pushed my shorts around my thighs and I was flashing the world."

Jace snorts and slaps the kitchen bench. "Shit."

"Yeah. Worst is they videotaped it and tried to sell us the memory."

"Oh, God, please say you bought it!"

"Are you kidding?"

He laughs harder. We share a couple more experiences we'd rather forget, and Jace excuses himself to the bathroom. When he comes back, he's carrying a plate of chocolate-lava cake and two forks. "Love chocolate," he says. "Couldn't miss this. Want some?"

I take the offered fork and we dig in.

"Did you come here with someone?" Jace asks with a token glance at the guests.

"No. Single. You?" I hold a forkful of cake to my lips.

"Me too."

I eat the cake and hold his gaze longer than before. He rests his fork on the plate and I follow suit. I pick at my shirt and undo a button. "It's stuffy in here. You want to go for a walk?"

"Sure."

I lead him outside through a gap in the trellises. When we hit the fringe of the bush, he stops and looks at me.

"This way," I say warmly.

Fern leaves comb our sides as we trek down the dark trail. Our steps make a dull clumping sound on the packed-dirt path.

Jace hesitates, and I pause with him. His mask reflects the strands of moonlight filtering through the trees. I can't be sure but I think a grin is pulling at his lips. "You can't expect me to follow you out into the bush in the middle of the night!"

The words stir an earlier memory—I think they were meant to. "And yet, here you are."

He follows me around the bend toward the babbling creek. If I listen closely enough, I think I'll hear our story being told to us.

Outside the cave, I stop. "We have to whisper now. Come."

He's close behind me as we move into the cave. For a moment, I linger in his warmth and observe his slow, sweet smile.

The glowworms seem brighter than ever. Maybe they're celebrating our return. "Been a long time since I've been out here."

"How long?" he whispers.

"Years."

I try to count the hundreds of pearly-green lights but like always, I don't finish.

Jace turns and walks out.

I leave a few moments after him. He's standing at the creek, touching his mask as if considering lifting it. He drops his hand. "Thank you for taking me here."

"Want to head back?"

He nods.

When we get back to the garden, we veer toward the nook at the end and sit on the bench dusted with real spider webs. The cool wood bites through my shirt.

I pull the hourglass stone from my pocket. Jace is watching me, so I hand it over to him. "I got this today."

His voice is on the cusp of breaking. "What is it?"

"I'm not sure," I say. "It could be anything."

"What do you think it is?"

"An apology. Or maybe someone misses me as much as I miss him."

His breath hitches.

I continue, "But I'm not sure that's possible."

"Why not?"

"Because the guy who gave this to me broke my heart. I've thought about him and missed him every day for five years. Every single day."

"Maybe it's the same for him?" He's staring at the stone in his hand.

"Maybe."

"Were you close?" He fiddles with the stone, not lifting his gaze to me.

"We used to hang out as kids in the cave."

His eyes close. I pluck the stone from his warm hands and slide it back into my pocket. "It's cold, let's get back to the reception."

Back inside, we sidle up to the bar and order two more whiskeys. It fuels the nervous flare in my belly and shoots shivers to the tips of my fingers and toes. The mask is heavy against my nose and I adjust it.

"I like it," he says. "Your mask."

I laugh. "I hope that's not all you like."

"No."

The direct response sobers me.

Ice numbs my hand where I clutch my glass. I sip, staring at the wait staff as they rush to pour drinks and clean spills.

His gaze burns the side of my face like the whiskey burns

my throat.

"What are you thinking about, Wesley?"

He holds out a hand. "Would you like to dance, Mr. Son of the Groom?"

My breath catches. "Call me Cooper."

He wraps his warm hand around my iced one and leads me to the dance floor.

Tens of couples are waltzing. Among them, Annie and Ernie are sharing a tender kiss. Lila and Dad are at the sidelines pointing at people's feet and discussing something.

Jace tugs my arm just enough to turn me. He slides closer, placing his right hand on my waist toward my back. I set my hand on his shoulder. He steps forward into a simple waltz and falters. "Sorry, did you want to lead?"

"I don't mind. I'm versatile."

His lips twitch. "Me too but if you prefer—"

"Lead. Please."

His steps are confident but his eyes hold a vacant sheen.

The first song ends and the next starts. I squeeze his shoulder. "You know the guy I told you about?"

"The one who you think gave you the stone?"

I don't step back as far on the next beat, drawing us an inch closer. "The one I *know* gave me the stone."

"What about him?" His words hit my neck and tunnel under my collar.

"He's a musician. A brilliant musician."

His grip tenses. "Is he?"

"Yes. You might have heard him play and sing with my sister earlier."

"I'd hardly call the performance brilliant."

I smile. "He plays as an accompaniment to operas, ballet, and modern dance. Even had an appearance with the Dunedin orchestra."

"Just classical stuff? Sounds pretentious."

"He's not though. He makes crowds cry. Makes them roar for more."

He blinks. "Is that right?"

"Yes. I know. I've been to every concert he's ever done."

He misses a step. "Sorry, I—"

"You okay?"

He holds my gaze then steers me back into the waltz. His tender touch prickles my skin with goosebumps. "Why would you see his concerts if he broke your heart?"

"He means too much to me not to witness his successes."

"You saw all of them?"

"Yes." I whisper at his ear. "And they were brilliant."

He shivers and presses us closer with each step. "That's amazing of you."

"Do you think he would have minded if he knew I was there?"

"I think he'd have been touched. I imagine he wishes he'd invited you in the first place."

"But he didn't."

"The guy is a fool."

"I wonder if he's changed but doesn't know how to tell me?"

"Can he be both a fool and have changed?"

"I don't think so."

"Maybe he's between the two—no longer a fool because he knows what he's done wrong, but he hasn't quite figured out how to change either."

"Do you think he eventually will?"

Jace shrugs.

Lila and Dad are scaring half the dancers with their awkward steps. The song winds down, and I pull out of Jace's grasp. "Another drink, Wesley?"

"Please."

"I'll grab them and we can go somewhere quiet. Sound good?"

His Adam's apple juts as he swallows and nods.

When I come back with two whiskeys, I lead him upstairs to the balcony. The music rises faintly from below but otherwise it's quiet.

We huddle together in the fresh breeze, our drinks resting on the flat wooden edge of the railing. The bush we walked through is a dark silhouette against a star-spotted sky.

"I think you might be right."

"What's that?"

"My guy isn't really mine right now." I face him and he mirrors me. "I'm glad I met you tonight, Wesley."

His gaze runs over my mask to my nose and lingers on my mouth. "You are?"

I draw closer. "Perhaps you can help me show my man what he's missing."

His breath catches and his gaze flickers to mine. "What did you have in mind?"

"If we were"—I slide my hands down his hips and draw us together until our hard groins meet—"to get close like this." My voice drops to a whisper. "Maybe we could make him jealous of you."

"And if it doesn't work?"

"Then I had a wonderful night with this incredibly hot guy named Wesley, friend of the bride—"

He kisses me. Our masks and noses bump, and his lips press firmly against mine, sucking in my bottom lip. His arms draw tight around me and I moan into the kiss, deepening it with my tongue. I press my groin against his and lightly thrust while I cup the back of his neck and massage him closer.

He shifts, his thigh slipping between mine, and suddenly I'm passionately shoved against the railing and one of our glasses falls and cracks on the grass below. "God, you're beautiful," he says, rubbing his nose against mine and staring into my eyes before resuming our kiss. "But I can't do this," he says as his kisses trail over my jaw and under my ear. "I can't. It's not fair to you."

"Of course you can, Wesley," I say. "You're just a one-night stand. I know not to expect you in the morning."

"That's not right," he says again, but his hands explore my back and he holds me so close his heart hammers against my chest.

"Please don't stop," I whisper.

"Cooper—"

"Please."

He hesitates for a fraction of a second, like he's trying with every ounce of restraint to pull back but he can't. His warm lips crush against mine once more and his fingers tickle as he drags them up my neck to thread into my hair.

A cool breeze hits my back, and with it, I push us back to the balcony door and through to my bedroom.

The lights are off and it's dark, but we stumble to my bed, kick off our shoes and yank down our pants while locked in kisses. The heat of his hard cock nudges mine, and the length of his thigh presses warmly between my legs. I thrust against him, eliciting an animalistic groan.

His fingers are trembling just as mine are as we fumble to undo the buttons on each other's shirts. His comes off first and drops to the floor.

Jace rearranges his cock so it's between my thighs, rubbing lightly at my balls. He finishes the last button and sweeps his hands over my shoulders and down my arms until my shirt hits his. His full length is against mine, everything hot save the cool bite of his greenstone hook jammed between our chests.

I maneuver us to my side table where I pull out supplies. I'm aching to have him inside me, and I make quick work of rolling on the condom and lathering him with lube. I poured too much on my hand and Jace scoops some up on his fingers as he takes my cock in his hand and strokes me lovingly.

His lube-laced fingers draw over my balls and press tantalizingly against my entrance. I want—need—more. I lie lengthwise on the bed and Jace crawls on top of me. His hand gently probes my ring as he kisses and suckles my nipple. His mask scratches the top of my shoulder, reminding me to bite down on crying out his name.

This is Wesley. Tonight, he's Wesley.

No, he's not.

Now who's the fool?

"Please," I say, after he's thoroughly worked me with his

fingers.

He kisses a path up my stomach to my chin, and the hook bumps along my skin with them.

I grip his cock, angling it at my entrance. He sucks in a pant and kisses me hard.

"Please," I say again as the head of his cock pushes into me. "All I want is you."

He slides all the way in and I grab his hips as I arch against him. He stills and presses his forehead against my ear, his harsh breath tickling my neck. "Cooper."

I swallow the rise of emotion and focus on how full I feel, how my cock is rubbing against his skin, how my toes are curling, the way the silky bed sheets feel against the back of my thighs.

I dig my fingers into his hips. He snaps into a thrust that jolts me with deliciousness I need more of.

He thrusts into me like a waltz, three times and the swivel of his hips, over and over until I hear the music and feel it beating against my skin.

He kisses me again, and closes a hand around my cock.

I clench at the pleasure and we both let out a groan. His thrusts push me closer and closer to the edge. I want to fall so badly but I don't want this to be over. Never want this to be over.

As if he can read my mind, he slows his thrusts but he doesn't let go of me. I fight not to give in to the pleasure of his strokes and the way his thumb brushes over the head.

He looks down at me, his jaw clenched in passion, but he never closes his eyes. His mask glitters but his eyes are pinning my soul to his. It's intimate in a way I've never experienced. I'm somewhere between panicking and experiencing the biggest release of my life.

He bites his lip and rocks more quickly into me. The bed groans with us, and I clutch Jace's ass tightly, pressing him in, in, in.

The strokes on my cock are in time to his and when he presses his mouth against mine and calls my name over my lips, I come with him, crying out as my orgasm bursts out of me and keeps coming, coming, coming.

malachite

I follow his blog through Germany, France, Spain, Greece, Turkey, and Scotland. I wish I'd thought to give him a piece of malachite to protect him on his travels.

Malachite, a copper carbonate hydroxide mineral.

Mineral. Not a protective talisman.

He's Jace, a pianist traveling the world before settling into a career of teaching.

His own person. Not *mine.*

Tonight, he posted about England.

I'm at Mum's for our weekly roast but I'm not hungry. Paul offers me the carafe of gravy, but drowning the dry vegetables isn't going to make a difference. I pick at the chicken and eat a few peas. After a bite of potato, I rest my knife and fork on the plate.

Mum eyes me, questioningly arching an eyebrow. "Ever since you started flatting, you've neglected your diet."

"I'm not hungry right now," I murmur. I ask Annie where Ernie is tonight.

Mum cuts over her answer. "It's not just now. You haven't been hungry in months and you're studying yourself thin." She turns to Annie. "Get your boy to take this one out on a guys' night. I think he needs it."

"What I need," I say, shoving my chair back from the table, "is to bloody well be in England."

I walk out. Everything is winding me up the wrong way—

even the way the bus driver gave me a cheery greeting earlier. No, I won't have a good day, dammit.

My days are restless as though ants are marching through my veins, tickling my insides so I can't settle.

I stop in my bedroom doorway. It looks smaller than it used to. Even the toolboxes lining the walls don't seem to have the presence they once had. I breathe in the stale air, then turn my back on the younger me and head outside.

The veranda creeks underfoot, and the winter air bites as I hunker down, resting against the house. I pull out my phone.

England, Stonehenge

A picture with a short caption underneath:
Something's missing.

I rub my phone over my forehead, trying to smooth out the heavyset frown that seems to be staining itself to my skin.

The wooden planks creak, and I glance up. Mum is shrugging on a brown winter coat and stealing toward me. She sighs and drops down next to me, draping a green mohair scarf around my neck.

"It's Jace, isn't it?"

"What?"

She takes my phone and slips it into her pocket. "You miss him."

I knock my head back against the side of the house and stare at the quarter moon. "It's complicated."

"Ah," she says in that all-knowing tone that mothers have. "I see." I drop my head to her shoulder, and she pats my head in that awkward way she does.

"It's okay," she says. For a second, the stars look like the glowworms in our cave. "It's not like you're real brothers."

apache tear drop

It is said those who have an Apache Tear Drop will never cry again.

Legend speaks of a brutal surprise attack on the Apaches, where fifty of seventy-five men were shot. The remaining twenty-five retreated to the edge of the cliffs, where they chose to jump rather than be killed as their brothers were.

The Apache women, lovers, mothers, sisters, and daughters gathered at the base of the cliff and mourned their loved ones. Their sorrow was so great that their tears turned to black stones.

Holding this stone to the light reveals the shimmer of the Apache Tear Drop and is good luck to those who have it. They will never cry again because the Apache cried enough for them.

I hold this stone after learning that Lila's cancer has returned.

I hold it after learning that the cancer has spread to her bone marrow, lungs, and liver.

I hold it after watching Dad cry that it's the liver that will take her away from us in a few months.

I hold it after overhearing Dad telling Jace to cut his trip short and come home.

I hold it after Annie hugs him, me, then Lila who is sitting on the grass outside in the spot her and Dad were married.

I hold it but it doesn't take any pain away.

The Apache women did not cry enough for Lila.

Annie brings over the kauri rocking chair I gave her. She smiles at me in the doorway to the dining room as Lila sinks onto the cushions.

The patio doors are open and a warm breeze stirs the trees and ruffles Lila's skirt. She grips the chair arms and rocks. "This is lovely, Annie."

Dad squeezes Annie into a hug and slips into the kitchen to make tea. His back is to me and his shoulders are higher up than usual, as though he's stiff with worry.

I push off the doorway to help him when the doorbell rings.

"I'll get that."

For all the windows in this house, it is strange that the door is so solid, so dark, so impenetrable. I grip the cool handle, ready to let him in.

I pull the door open.

Jace stands in the porch with his suitcase and carry-on bag. He's tanner than the last time I saw him at Lila and Dad's wedding, but unlike the suave suit he wore then, he's wearing jeans stained with flight food and wine. Even with sunglasses on, the puffiness of his cheeks gives his tears away.

"You're home," I choke out.

He doesn't move forward to hug me or even push past me. It's as though he's afraid to cross the threshold of truth.

I pick up his suitcases and drag them inside. They're

heavy with a hundred memories of fun and laughter.

"I'll put these in your room."

He stops me, finally breaching the threshold. "Wait. I have something in there for her."

Jace unzips the front pocket of his large bag and pulls out a small box. He hops to his feet, sliding his sunglasses onto his head. Tears have made his eyes a shocking blue. "Where is she?"

"The dining room, by the patio."

He clutches his gift and heads toward his mum.

I move his stuff to his room and head downstairs.

Dad is still standing in the kitchen with his back to us, even though the water is well and truly boiled. Annie is on the patio watering the potted plants, and Jace is placing a pendant over his mum's head.

"What is it?" she asks.

"Stonehenge bluestone." A precious stone used for centuries in alternative healing. "It'll help you get better."

A cup drops and smashes on the floor. I hurry into the kitchen to help dad clean it up. It's my cup he dropped—my Rock Whisperer one. Though it's beyond saving, I stow the pieces in a freezer bag anyway.

Dad is sitting on the floor leaning against a cupboard. I crouch next to him and rest a hand on his knee, rubbing the linen.

"Come with me," I tell him. "The afternoon, just you and I." Let Lila have time with her son to break it to him in her way.

"Yeah," Dad says, running a hand through his greying hair. "That's probably a good idea."

We hike the ridges of the hills where pine needles sweeten the air. Birds click and cackle and wheeze overhead. I wonder if they are conversing about us:

They seem rather somber, don't they?

Like they built a nest in the shadows and have never see the sun.

Poor things. Someone should teach them how to fly.

A white-tufted bird with dark, iridescent feathers swoops in front of us, bringing us to a sudden halt in the middle of a patch of sun. “Jesus, that was close.”

I spin in an arc to find the bird again. I spot its black opal feathers in the tree to our left. “It was a Tui.”

Tui. Tui. Tui. The word is mimicked back to us. Yep, definitely a Tui. “Hear that? It’s incredible.”

Dad nods. “Sounded just like you. Lila would be beside herself. She loves Tuis.”

She loves Tuis. She loves Tuis. She loves Tuis.

And it sounds a bit like *She loves you, eh*?

Dad laughs, his crow’s feet deepening. “That’s beautiful.”

He slings an arm around my shoulders and kisses my temple.

That’s beautiful. That’s beautiful. That’s beautiful. The bird says.

It is.

smoky quartz

At home, Jace is pulling ingredients out of the fridge and pantry for dinner. Lila sits in her rocking chair with a notepad and a pen, letting ink flow over the fine blue lines as she writes. Dad kisses her cheek and she stops writing to ask what we did. She laughs as I draw in a breath and move into the kitchen.

Jace.

He glances up at me and steps to the side, offering me space next to him. But he doesn't say anything. I take a cutting board and a sharp knife, then take over cutting the onions. They sting my eyes but I'm used to that now. I dice until Jace is ready for them.

They sizzle when they hit the pan. Jace stirs them into the butter with a long wooden spoon and languid strokes, cutting into the onions like he's writing something of his own.

"How was Europe?" I ask when the mushrooms are frying and the pasta is boiling. I cock the lid of the pot so the water doesn't bubble over.

"Good for me."

"Better than home?"

He stops stirring and looks me squarely in the eyes. "I know we have to talk." He swallows and looks toward his mum and our dad. "But can you wait?"

I can. I have. I always will.

When dinner is ready, Dad calls down Annie and Ernie and

we all sit around the table and eat.

Lila smiles at each of us, winking at Ernie, who blushes the color of the roses in the middle of the table.

Lila eats a few mouthfuls more than she has the past couple of days. "This tastes great, Jace. Mushroom and capsicum cream sauce?"

"The very one you taught me."

I poke at the pasta Jace served me, preparing to pull out all the capsicums before I dig any more into it.

I frown at Jace twirling his pasta on his fork.

You took out the capsicum for me, didn't you?

Ernie clears his throat. "Hey, Jace."

"Yeah?"

"Knock-knock."

Jace raises an eyebrow. "Who's there?"

"Amish."

"Amish who?"

"Aww, I missed you too."

Annie claps him over the back of the head. "Ernie!"

Dad and Lila laugh, and Jace grins too for the first time since coming home. I could kiss that dumb joke to bits; it's like smoky quartz—immediately relieving the tension in the room.

"I have another one," Ernie says as he swivels to face Annie. "Knock knock."

A short laugh. "Who's there?"

"Olive."

"Olive who?"

"Olive you too." Lila holds her breath and Annie smiles. Ernie pushes his chair back and kneels on one knee. He pulls a velvet box out of his pocket and opens it. Annie gasps. "Will you marry me?"

Annie bites her lip and throws her arms around his neck, knocking him backward until the chair behinds him tips and they are on the floor, laughing.

"Is that a yes?"

"Olive to marry you."

Dad leans over and kisses Lila's glowing face. I stand up on shaky legs, and everything is blurry as I round the table. Annie and Ernie are pulling themselves off the floor, and when my sister is on her two feet, I lift her into a hug and twirl her around. Her laugh puffs against my ear. "I'm so happy," she says and squeezes me back.

I set her down and invite Ernie into a man-hug with three quick thumps on the back. "Welcome to the family. Remember what I said to you at the Halloween-birthday-masquerade wedding?"

He snorts at the mouthful. "Like I could forget."

Dad pipes up. "Remember what I said too."

"Said?" Ernie cries out. "You *demonstrated* what you'd do."

"Yeah, but if you break your promise, the next time it won't be with props."

Dad is scary when he wants to be.

I laugh and hug him too. I breathe in the smell of pine on his clothes. "Jesus," he says, "you're all growing up. Next you and Jace will be engaged as well."

I know he doesn't mean engaged together but my heart skips a beat. Jace is hugging his mum but he's looking at me.

"Thank you, Ernie," Lila says when Jace pulls away. "I wish you and Annie a bright, beautiful future. Maybe you'll even give this one grandchildren one day," she says, pinching Dad's butt.

He jumps and scowls at Ernie. "Not for a long, long time."

Lila smiles, taking Dad in. "He'll be a wonderful granddaddy." She looks at Jace and me. "They'll be the best uncles, too."

Jace ducks out of the dining room and pounds up the stairs.

Lila makes a move to stand but Dad pats her shoulder. "Give the boy some time. He's jetlagged and tired. He needs his space."

I duck out as soon as I can, racing up to the gaming room where he's playing something soft on the piano.

When he finishes, he faces me. "Bit rusty," he says. "Haven't been practicing as much as I should."

"Sounds good to me."

"Are you living here?"

I incline my head. "Staying in a flat wasn't working out for me. Thought I'd camp here again for a while."

This isn't the whole truth. I came home with my bags last weekend. Lila's going to stay at home for the end and I want to be here.

"Me too," Jace says, closing the lid to the piano and standing.

"Guess that makes us neighbors again."

"Like the old days."

"But without switching houses."

He crosses the room and for a moment I think he's going to stroke my cheek but he rubs his eyes. "I'm glad of that." He yawns. "I really need to sleep."

We step into the hall and make our way to our rooms. Our gazes flicker to the balcony before we each crack our doors open.

"Good night, Jace."

"Night, Cooper."

I drop lengthwise onto my bed, gripping my bedcovers. Breathing in the stillness, I replay the night of the infamous Halloween-birthday-masquerade wedding.

Dad stays at Lila's side reading to her, playing games, watching movies, and taking naps with his fingers entwined with hers. As the weeks pass into months, he wells up with tears every time he walks into their room. He sleeps less and takes daily shots of port in his study.

I take over the rocking chair at her bedside, giving Dad the time he needs to pull himself together. I understand though. Lila has lost so much weight, and her gaunt face is lined with pain that her meds can't entirely take away. She tries to eat for us but she doesn't want to. She only wants to sleep.

And then a surge of energy overcomes her.

This morning she decided she needed to vacuum the carpets.

A strange beacon of hope coiled itself tightly in my gut. Could the doctors have gotten it all wrong?

I feel Dad's hysterical laughter and see his hand searching for hers at the dining table as they share a yogurt.

Then she curls up in bed like she does every normal day.

Dad hasn't left his study since.

"It's hard for him to see me like this," Lila says.

"And it's not hard for me?"

She pokes her tongue out. "I'm the witch that stole your father. Think of this as payback."

I sober. "No, Lila. A long time ago I was angry but it's been a long while now that I"—*love you*—"have come to like you a fair bit."

She laughs but it comes with a wince.

I rock in the chair as we listen to Jace's hectic music leaking through the walls. Three, four, five songs pass before Lila speaks again. When she does, it's hushed.

"What's the matter, Cooper?"

I meet her concerned blue gaze, which is so much like Jace's it makes me tremble. "Nothing."

She shakes her head and stares up at the lampshade, spinning from the vibrations of his music. "You wear your emotions on your sleeve. You've been sad ever since Jace came home."

I let out a rough laugh. "You think Jace is the one making me sad?"

"Yes. I think it's my boy that touches your heart the most."

The music seems to swell, seems to fill the room and turn my skin to shivers. "I don't know what you're talking about."

"I'm a dying woman. I have no time for lies."

I shut my eyes and a tear escapes. My throat feels like it's been scratched with a thousand toothpicks.

Lila continues, "You used to be so close. Right from the beginning, you and my son sparked." My breath shudders. Lila's voice softens. "He used to look at you like you held the answers to all life's mysteries. When you were doing dishes, he'd sit at the table longer just to watch you. When you were at your mum's, I'd find him curled in your bed holding one of your stones."

"He did that?"

"Yes."

This conversation feels like a confession. I'm afraid of what she might say, yet it's exactly what I long to know the most. When she doesn't say anything for a long time, I clutch the arms of the rocking chair and ask, "Is Dad Jace's father too?"

Stunned silence.

Lila gasps out something akin to a laugh. "Of course not!"

But she took too long to answer. I don't believe her. But she has no time for lies, right?

We look at each other for a long time, but she's guarding

her secrets well.

"Hypothetically," I say during the silent moment in the music. "If he were Jace's real dad, would you tell them?"

Again, she waits too long to answer. "Of course. They'd want to know."

"Would they?"

She smiles.

The music vibrates through the floor with a violently hopeful beat, then tinkers to something soft and sorrowful.

"Do me a favor?" Lila asks. "Tell him to play something jolly."

"We all grieve in our own way. This is his love song to you. It wouldn't feel right asking him to stop."

Tears streak down her temples and over her ears. She struggles to sit up. I plump a pillow behind her, and she grabs my wrist, rubbing her thumb over my skin. "I love you, Cooper. I know you have a mum but I have one secret to share with you."

"What's that?" I ask, kissing her forehead.

"You are mine as well." She lets go of me. "Don't tell him to stop but don't let him play my song too long. There are others he should be playing."

quartzite

Mum asks me to drive her, two casseroles and a coconut cake to Dad's.

I pull up outside the house. Sunlight reflects off the windows and bounces onto the neglected lawn, making it eerily bright. The straight lines and glass have dated over the years. What once screamed *We're better than you* now whispers *Things change.*

And haven't they?

Mum stares out the passenger window. The light mirrors her freckled face and grim smile.

"You don't have to go in," I say, rubbing my thumbs over the steering wheel.

"I want to." She glances down at the cake on her lap. White and square with a glassy luster like she dunked it in fine grains of sugar. It looks solid, like it might score a seven on the Mohs scale. A chunk of quartzite can withstand all pressure.

Mum sighs. "I just need to pray."

"You don't believe in God."

"Sometimes I do."

"What are you praying for?" Nothing can be done. *Please don't make me hope.*

"For forgiveness."

I drop my hands. Before I can ask, she speaks. "All those years ago when it didn't work out with your dad and I?"

"When he left?"

"Yes. No, before that. During our arrangement." Her breath hitches. "I wished something bad would happen to her. I didn't mean it, not really. But now I'm sorry I ever thought that."

Annie and I did the same thing.

I open our seatbelts and take the casseroles and quartzite coconut cake while she climbs out of the car. My belly is twisting at the sympathy I see in Mum's tight smile. "Let's go see your father."

We walk up the path bridging the grassy moat, each of us holding a lukewarm casserole in our trembling grasp.

As I fish for my keys, I cradle the casserole under one arm. I'm unlocking the door but it opens before I finish. Dad is staring at Mum.

"Hello, David."

"Marie. It's been a long time." He runs a hand through his hair and steps back to let us in.

Mum steps inside. "Too long."

Dad can't seem to stop nodding.

"Pass me the food, Mum."

She blinks. "Cake is for now. You can freeze the casseroles for up to four months."

I'm moving toward the kitchen when Mum's heels clack over the floor. She mutters, "I am so sorry. You are both in my prayers."

Dad gives a soft laugh, "You don't believe in God."

The house groans as I step into the dining room. *Things change.*

Mum's voice trails behind me, soft and comforting. "Like father, like son."

soapstone

"Hop in."

I lean over the passenger seat and open the door. Clutching a bunch of mail, Jace stares at me through the open passenger window.

I'd just come home from university and driven up the driveway. When I saw him, I had to get him in the car. "Come on."

He pulls the door open and slides in, gently tossing the mail on the dashboard. I rest a hand on the back of his seat and reverse swiftly out of the driveway.

He focuses on the view of the city as we wind down the hill toward the beach.

"Paua Shell Bay?" he asks, shuffling through the mail—again.

"Just like we used to."

More shuffling. "Fish and chips?"

"Are you hungry?"

His breath comes out heavier than the last ones. "You have no idea how hungry I am."

I go a touch heavy on the brakes and we jerk forward, belts tightening. "Sorry." His expression is unreadable. Unreadable, but tired. "I'm hungry too."

His gaze slips to my mouth but he quickly looks out the passenger window.

We park at the bay. We stuff the fish and chips under our parkas, zipped only halfway. We toe off our shoes and leave them at the car.

Salty breezes whip our hair and seagulls squawk overhead, flying over the low tide for anything to scavenge. Our feet sink into wet sand as we walk along the edges of the tide. Every few steps, the cool ocean bites our ankles. Jace is staring toward the horizon and the dark clouds drifting toward us.

The promise of rain is in the air but neither of us hurry. So what if we get wet? *We're not made of sugar*, Lila would say.

My fingers are greasy from the chips but the salt is delicious and I lick it off my thumb and forefinger.

I've finished my scoop but I could eat another. "Jace?"

He turns toward me, weary, as if he's not ready to talk yet.

I step closer, locking our gazes and feeling the warmth tingle between us. I dunk my hand down his jacket into his scoop of chips and pinch a handful.

"Hey!" he says with a relieved chuckle. "You had yours."

"Yeah, but I'm *really* hungry."

He sucks in a gulp of air just as a few drops of rain hit my nose and cheek. "Cooper—"

A loud squawk.

A seagull swoops down and boldly perches on Jace's forearm, ducking his head into the chips. Jace stands there, shocked, staring at me as if begging me to get rid of it.

I laugh so hard that my vision blurs, and my attempts to shoo the bird are shoddy at best. The rumbling thunder finally sends the seagull on his way and turns the smattering of raindrops into a torrent.

Rain drenches our hair and slips down our necks and under our shirts. It soaks through our clothes but we just stand here and let it.

I can't stop laughing, pointing at him, the bird, his face. "The seagull's hungry too!"

Water splashes into my open mouth and it tastes fresh, revitalizing. Just like the smile quirking at Jace's lips.

lodestone

My spiral-bound master's dissertation stares at me from the passenger seat of my car, the plastic cover winking at me in the autumn afternoon light.

"I'll read it," Dad said. "So long as you dedicate it to me."

I undo my belt and open the door. Breezes ruffle the pages, flicking them open to the title page. I pull it onto my lap, and fold it back one more page. It's not dedicated to Dad but I think he'll be more pleased this way.

My dissertation is not a rock. It will not last forever, protecting her name and memory, but it is one of the stepping stones of my life, and I want her to know . . . want her to know . . .

I clutch the work to my chest and jump out of the car.

The distant sounds of laughter startle me, and I follow them over the moat to the back yard.

Dad has a soccer ball aimed at Ernie, who raises his hands to protect his face. "I haven't done anything to your daughter!" he screams. "I swear she's still a virgin. Now stop trying to kill me with the round, padded object. I don't deserve to be taken this way."

Dad laughs. "Open your eyes, doofus. I'm kicking it to you, not at you."

Ernie reluctantly pulls his hands from his face and stares suspiciously at Dad.

I hover in the shadows at the edge of the house.

It's been a long time since Dad has laughed. I miss it. Miss the way he jerks his head back slightly and squishes his nose, lines deepening around his eyes. Like Ernie, he's wearing training pants and a long-sleeved shirt. Unlike Ernie's, Dad's shirt is rated PG.

Dad finally kicks the ball. Ernie steps out of the way instead of stopping it with his foot and it rolls to the house.

"I got it," Ernie says, jogging over to pick it up.

"It's a lost cause, Dad." I follow Annie's voice to the other side of the lawn, where she's spraying the garden.

"I heard that," Ernie says, positioning the ball at his feet and taking a few steps backward. "All right, David, here's a taste of your own medicine."

He puts energy into his kicks and swings his arms like a pro, except his foot catches the ball at the wrong angle. The ball smacks Annie in the back of the head.

A horrified gasp. Ernie races over to Annie, who has dropped her hose and is glaring. "Okay, kill me now with the round, padded object," Ernie says.

Dad drops to the grass. His laugh bellows out of him so hard, he's holding his ribs. "You okay, Annie?" he manages between bouts.

Annie is okay, just a little miffed—and confused which of the two idiots to scowl at. Soon, however, even her narrowed eyes are twinkling and she's chuckling along with them.

Ernie hugs her tightly, rubbing her back, working his fingers up to the nape of her neck. "Sorry," he says and kisses her. "For me, soccer is a spectator sport."

She grins and looks over at Dad, who's consumed with hysteria and sprawled out on the grass. She frowns and bites her lip.

I push away from the side of the house and walk over to him. His laugh is still pulling at his body but the sounds have broken and are silent. He stares past me at the sunset streaking the sky orange, red, and pink.

I lie next to him, hugging my dissertation. Annie and Ernie

join us until we are one big compass. Dad, north. Me, east. Annie, south. Ernie, west. Breezes stir, and it's like we are lying on lodestones, a natural magnetic iron ore that makes the needle spin wildly, jerking back and forth, and none of us know which direction it will land.

When Dad sniffs, I shuffle closer. We'll figure out where to go from here. I know we will be okay. "She loves Tui, remember?"

His sob returns to a laugh. "She loves you, eh?"

We lie like this until I glance toward the house and catch Jace leaning with his elbows on the side of the balcony, looking down at us. He's too far away for me to guess what he's thinking.

He's too far away. He should be here too.

Still holding my dissertation, I sit up slowly. The back of my shirt is damp from the cool grass.

"How about I race out with Annie and grab us some take out?" Ernie says.

Dad starts to protest that Lila won't be able to join in—but then he nods. "Yeah. That'd be great." He spots what I'm holding and points. "What's this?"

I pass it to him. "My dissertation."

He flips through the hundred and fifty pages, and then shakes his head. "You get your brains from your mum. This looks impressive." He flips to the dedication page. He swallows then claps the dissertation shut and hands it back to me, cupping the back of my neck and leading me inside the house. "I'm proud of you, Cooper."

"Thanks, Dad."

"I'm going to run up and show Lila."

"Do that."

No music greets me when I run upstairs, and a quick peek at the balcony reveals Jace has left. I want to find him first to show him my work; I want to be near him for a few moments but he's not in his room, either, so I head to Lila's.

I stop right outside Lila's door when I hear Jace speaking in her room.

"I mean, I don't know—" I sneak a look through the open

door. Pillows prop Lila up and she's rubbing the bluestone necklace as if it were rosary beads.

Jace sits forward on the rocking chair, hands clasped and resting at her side. He stares at the stone too.

"It's okay, Jace."

"No, it's not. You're meant to be here."

I flatten my back against the hall wall, then slide down until I'm sitting. I thumb the pages of my dissertation as I eavesdrop.

"I can't keep having this conversation," she says quietly. "It takes too much energy. All I want is for you to be happy. Can you do that? Can you be brave for me?"

A long pause.

"You're right, Mum. I'm sorry." He plants a quick kiss on her. "I want that too."

"Tell me more about your travels. What was the stupidest thing you did?"

"Cheers, Mum."

She chuckles. "Come on, then, spit it out."

"I could never figure out the underground toll gates so I kept banging into them rather than through them. Looked like a right idiot."

"Bet you did."

A laugh.

"I also left my luggage in a bus in Edinburgh and spent the next two days tracking it down."

"That sucks."

"But I had to find it because I had valuables in there."

"Anything else? Come on, something embarrassing!"

"You're cruel."

"My job."

"Fine. I almost got robbed in Rome. Some guy had my backpack and was heading out of the train. I grabbed my suitcase and started running after him, yelling for him to give it back. Well, it turned out I was wearing my backpack."

Another soft laugh.

"In my defense, I was jetlagged as hell."

“That has to be the stupidest thing,” she says.

Pause. “It’s not though.”

“What was then?”

The rocking chair creaks and thumps against the wall.

“It’s okay,” Lila says. “You don’t have to tell me everything. What was the best part of your trip?”

“Finding this,” he says, followed by a rustle of movement.

Lila whispers so it’s hard to catch. “Beautiful. Where did you find it?”

Jace whispers too softly for me to make out.

“Want to watch a movie?”

“Yeah, Jace. I’d love that. So long as it has a happily ever after.”

rhodochrosite

After the nurse tells us to prepare for Lila's passing in the next few weeks, Jace disappears into the bush, which glows with pale morning light.

I shove my feet into a pair of Dad's old shoes—the nearest available—and chase after him.

He must have broken into a run because I can't see him through the gaps in the trees. I follow the creek around the bend to the cave.

He's inside, huddled in the corner, his heavy breathing strained. For a moment, we're kids again, and I'm looking at myself panicking in the closet. But Jace lifts his head and fast-forwards me twelve years.

I kneel next to him and rub his back. "It'll be okay. We'll make it through this. We're a team: you, me, Annie, and Dad."

"Because we're family," Jace says.

"Because we love each other."

His breath hitches. He takes a long few minutes to stop trembling. When he does, he leans back against the smooth, damp wall and rolls his neck until he's looking at me.

It's dark in the cave, but not as dark as when we come out at night; the glowworms don't seem to glow as much either.

"I want to forget everything, Cooper. Maybe laugh again. Just for a day."

"Okay," I say. *I'll give you laughter in times of sadness.* "I promise."

* * *

I think quickly, and half an hour later, I tell Dad I'm stealing Jace for the day and we'll be back in the evening. He raises a brow then nods, watching me prepare a daypack with the essentials: water, food, and a picnic blanket.

I pull Jace from the loneliness of his room, my hand wrapped firmly around his wrist. "We're going hiking."

"Now?"

"Now."

In ten minutes, we're hurtling down the street toward adventure. An hour later, we arrive at Rimutaka Forest Park.

We pile out of the car, and I strap the daypack on. We've been quiet during the drive, but the contemplative quiet. The one that heals.

We hike through the bush, chasing our shadows over a long, narrow swing bridge, and over hills to the valley.

It's late afternoon and few words have passed between us when our feet hit the rocky river edge. I lead him over the rocks, to a stretch where the stones are smaller, shifting under our steps.

Surrounded by majestic hills, a glittering river, and sun-warmed stones beneath us, this is the perfect spot.

I stop and so does Jace. He breathes in deeply as I take off my backpack, pull out a blanket and lay it over a bed of pebbles. The stones sink with us as we sit, but it's comfortable the way they mold to our position.

I pull out leftovers from last night's dinner—macaroni and cheese.

I hand him a fork and scoot closer so we can share. Our forks clink as we shovel down the pasta. It's cold, but cheesy and delicious.

Jace drops some on his pants, pinches the insubordinate pasta and pops it into his mouth, licking this thumb. When we're done eating, he casually rests his elbows on his knees and watches a flock of birds lift into flight and disperse in the sky.

He sighs and speaks softly, “I asked Mum about my dad.”

I wrap my arms around myself, hoping futilely to contain a shiver. “And?”

Jace scrubs his face, and his fingers drift over his forehead and dig into his hair. Toward his knees, he continues, “She said she’s sorry that she can’t give me more details about him.”

I watch the river water carve its memories on the rocks below as Jace’s words carve into me.

His voice stumbles. “I asked her what his name was again. ‘Roger, right?’ I said, and Mum nodded. Said that was right. Roger.” His blue eyes brighten in the warm afternoon sun. “But there was never any Roger. I made up the name to see if she’d trip up, and she tripped.”

I let out a slow, uneven breath. “That doesn’t mean anything, Jace. The nurse said the last stages of cancer make it hard to remember things. People can get really confused.”

He’s staring at me but I can’t look at him. I don’t want to see the apology that might be there. The apology and the final goodbye to *us*.

“Confused,” he repeats, and I close my eyes. A half-hearted breeze stirs between us like it’s dying. Like it’s a sign.

“Let’s go,” I say. I resist the urge to throw a rock in the river.

“No.”

I open my eyes. Jace is shaking his head. “No. I’m not ready to go back yet. Another hour. Please.”

Another hour before we have to go home and face reality once more.

“Besides,” Jace says, putting on a brave smile. “I haven’t laughed yet.”

His sadness overwhelms me, and I yearn to eliminate it in any way possible.

“Lie down,” I tell him. He frowns slightly. “Trust me.”

He lies down.

“Close your eyes,” I say, feeling for small, flat pebbles. “Are they closed?”

“Yep.”

I crawl over to him and gently set one of the pebbles between his eyebrows. “Ideally this would be rhodochrosite, but concentrate on the weight and nothing else.”

“Roadoc—what now?”

I press lightly against the stone and draw back, careful not to graze him but keeping close. “Shhh. I’ll tell you later.”

Rhodochrosite. A magnesium carbonate mineral, light pink to reddish-pink, found in fractures of sedimentary and metamorphic rocks. A three or four on the Mohs scale.

The stone is used for healing loneliness, loss, a pained heart.

I keep still next to him, saying nothing, just admiring his smooth sun-kissed skin, the etches of humor at his eyes, the sharp angle of his nose, and his resting palms open in a show of complete trust.

After ten minutes, his lips curve into a curious grin. “Cooper?”

“Yeah?”

“What are we doing?”

“Did your skin prickle? Did you feel that rush like you do when you fall?”

He opens his eyes. “Are you sure that’s the stone?”

I lean forward, and our eyes lock. He breathes in as I breathe out, as though he’s pulling me closer. I press the stone against his forehead and a shiver rolls through his body.

Before I make a fool of myself, I remove the stone. “We should get going so we make it back before dark.”

Her birthstone.
They say rubies restore youth and vitality.
I say they lie.

Lila passes away two weeks later.

sapphire

At the funeral, our family comes forward one by one to say a few words.

Dad stands next to the closed casket and reads a letter Lila wrote him when he was eighteen and living in the States.

"It's a very short letter," he says, smiling at the yellowed note in his hand. "She sent it via airmail." He swallows a few times. "It says *I miss you.*"

He holds up the paper. "That's it, just those three words."

He turns to the casket and touches it. His silent cry racks his body and his voice comes out warbled. "I miss you too. I love you."

Annie sniffs next to me and I squeeze her hand tighter. Jace is on her other side and Annie is holding his hand too.

But Annie pulls away from us and helps steer Dad to the pew. Jace grabs him into a hug, but his eyes find mine over Dad's shoulder.

Annie clears her voice and speaks into the microphone. "For a long while, Lila and I didn't get along," she says. "I pushed her away and refused to acknowledge she was important to my dad." She looks over at us, lingering on Dad. "I am sorry for that, and I'm sorry I didn't appreciate her every day she was around. She was a clever, funny, intelligent woman, and I wish I had known her longer. None of us can know what the future will bring. Lila has taught me to love every day, and to love fiercely."

Jace goes up next but his words aren't said, they are sung and played on the grand piano set on the other side of the casket.

It's U2, because it was her favorite.

The church gives a collective sigh when he finishes. When he doesn't move from the piano stool, I wipe my tears and move over to him. I don't coax him off his stool; I sit next to him and pass him the stone I brought with me. Sapphire. "It's her favorite," I whisper in his ear. He clutches it.

Sitting in front of a sea of black dresses and suits, I pull out my speech and angle the microphone Jace used.

He's warm next to me as I flick through my cue cards. I squint but I can't read what I wrote. I stare at the mourners and focus on Dad and Annie.

Jace is leaning forward, resting his arms against his thighs, staring at the stone. His tears glisten as they fall onto the piano keys.

"She wasn't my mother." The words leap into the air and burst through the speakers to the far back of the church, where stained glass windows glow bright red and yellow.

I close my eyes and pray. Today I believe in God. Today I believe Lila can hear me. "You weren't my mum," I say again, "but you were mine too."

Jace stirs. When I open my eyes, he's looking right at me. His eyes are bright and he's trembling.

"It's true," he whispers. Though his words are for me, the microphone gifts them to the church.

"What is?" I ask, pushing the microphone away from us.

"This." He fingers the piano keys and starts playing. The chords choke a cry out of me. The song is so tender it hurts. It's as though Jace is holding my soul with his hands and kissing it.

He doesn't sing this time, just plays, but the words are there anyway.

It's too much. Everything.

And I—can't.

Can't process it.

Abruptly, I leave the piano stool and hurry back to our pew. I want to run out of here. I want to yell and shake him, but . . . Lila.

For Lila I stay strong.

I stare at my shoes. Stare at her polished casket. Stare into the air as if my next breath will give me the answers.

I feel Jace watching me but I do not acknowledge the complicated web of feelings. Not in the church. Not at the cemetery. Not at the wake.

When night falls and the house breathes its first sign of peace, I grab a jacket and head out the back door. A strong breeze stings my eyes and freeze-dries the tears at my temples and jaw.

I'm no fool. I know Jace is following me. The rustle of foliage and the crunch of his step tells me he isn't in a hurry to catch me.

I need to find a rock.

I stop outside our cave, at the edge of the creek. I sit on a flat boulder that rocks like a seesaw. I filter river stones through my fingers and look for the perfect one.

They're too big, too small, too chipped, too broken. None are right. None are what I need.

From the corner of my eye, I catch Jace approaching from the path to my side. He sits on the other side of my boulder, lifting up my side until we balance.

I adjust to the position and continue sifting stones through my fingers.

"It's true," he says quietly. The vibrations of his song play inside me, beating out its rhythm on my heart, in my gut, in my groin.

More stones slip through my fingers.

Jace takes the back of my hand and slowly threads his fingers through mine. Jace dips our hands into the cool stones until my hand is again full of brown and grey stones. But this time, they don't slide through my fingers because Jace's fingers are there to catch them.

The warmth of his hand under mine sends shivers to my fingertips and toes.

Jace gently brings my hand to his lap. One by one, he picks up the stones and drops them until only one is left.

Jace traces around the stone, tickling my palm. He stops circling and closes my hand around the stone. "This," he says, his voice cracking. "This is it."

My heart beats harder and I raise my head to look at him. His eyes are swollen from tears and grief but there's something else too. Something that glitters. Something that pulls more shivers out of me—

"I love you, Cooper," he says. "I am *in* love with you, and I have been since I was fifteen and we watched the glowworms together."

I look over his shoulder to the mouth of the cave.

His words draw me back. "The first moment I saw you, I knew my life would never be the same, though I didn't know how much until later."

He shifts enough to bring us closer, and the rock gently rolls. His tender gaze strokes my face.

"You are *my* rock." He squeezes my hand the way I squeezed his on the soccer field at Newtown High. "I wish I'd been brave enough to tell Mum that." His other hand cups the side of my face. I lean into it. "But you can bet I'm going to be brave enough from now on." He leans in and inhales deeply but stops on the cusp of a kiss. "Do I . . . do we . . . is there a chance for an us?"

"Our story never sank," I murmur. "The breezes carried it for us."

"Sorry?"

I turn my head and kiss his palm. "Yes."

"Yes?" He leaps up from the boulder and pulls me with him. "Yes?"

His sudden, deep laughter echoes in the stone still clasped in my hand. I'm laughing too. I grasp his wrist and tug him close. His breath catches and the laughter stops but the smile remains in the way he rakes over my face and lingers at my lips.

“Come,” he says, the words fanning over the side of my face and landing on the sensitive spot at my ear. “We have something we need to do.”

* * *

Jace unearths the brown envelope from his desk drawer and takes it out to our shared balcony. He rests it on the railing between us.

The tiny flap at the top of the envelope, where Jace and I tried opening it, winks in the moonlight.

“There’s too much weight between us.” He pulls out a lighter and flicks it on. The flame burns brightly, dancing orange and blue, twisting to the song of the wind. “But maybe we can make some of it go away?”

The flame bows and leaps. “You want to burn the truth?”

“No,” he says. “I want to finally *live* it. I had to travel the world to piece it all together, but the truth isn’t in this envelope.”

He’s waiting for me. He won’t do it unless I want it too. *Do you care?*

“I don’t care,” I say softly. “Whatever it says won’t change how I feel. How I’ve always felt. If it weighs on you, burn it.”

He picks up the edge and hesitates. “You’re right, it doesn’t matter.”

The light snaps off.

Jace shifts, fingers stroking the top flap. He wedges one finger under and slides it to the other side. The flap waves in another breeze. He dips his fingers in and starts to draw out the papers, but I cage his hand with mine.

What if he thinks it doesn’t matter now but later it does?

Do I want to risk that?

I free the lighter from his other hand and command the flame to rise once more. I do not hesitate. I draw his hand away and light the envelope. It catches the flame and it curls with the fire. Cinders break off and float away on a breeze.

We watch each other over the burning DNA results. My skin prickles from head to toe.

When there's nothing left except us and ash, relief washes away the tension in my shoulders.

Jace closes the distance, brings me in close, and wraps me in his warmth. We hug like this, shifting from foot to foot and nuzzling closer, closer—

I press a kiss under his ear. It's soft and light but only for a second. Jace stills.

We look into each other's eyes, and much like the first time, we stir up a whirlwind of passion. Kissing, touching, and stumbling to his bed, we collapse. Jace lays on top of me, kicks off his shoes and pushes mine off with his toes as he kisses me deeply.

Our cocks align and we rut against each other through our pants. Somehow I work off his jacket and our shirts.

He pulls me into a sitting position, straddling my hips. He kisses me once more and leans over to pull something out from under his bed.

I rest my forehead against his shoulder and kiss his upper arm. His skin pebbles against my lips.

"What are you doing?" I whisper.

He pulls out a mirrored mask from under the bed and dangles it between us. When it spins, it hits both our noses.

"This time when we make love," he says softly. "There'll be no pretending."

* * *

Raw, honest, naked. His hot skin presses against mine as we kiss. My fingers push through his hair, squeeze his neck and skate over his shoulder blades. I press him closer. His greenstone hook is cool between us, imprinting on my chest.

Jace is right. This is it.

Just us. No masks. No double meanings.

I suck on his neck, drawing in his scent to make it mine. My lips work up to his ear. Our hearts hammer like music.

I capture his ear lobe and tease it with my teeth. His hips swivel and his hard cock slides against mine. "I need to be close."

Jace pulls back enough to look down at me. The heat, passion, and need in his eyes reflects my own. A swelling tenderness—

He dips and kisses me lightly. "I need that too."

He kisses me again as he rips open the condom package. My cock throbs as he squeezes me and rolls it on. He's generous with the lube and takes his time stroking it onto me. I gasp at the firm, slick touch, and desire plows through me, jerking me up. I cup his neck and kiss him again, and push him down onto the bed. My mouth roams his chest, lightly biting his nipples. My fingers run through the lube at my cock and push at his entrance.

I'm impatient. Needy. I try to be gentle but I drive my fingers into him. He's pleading me for more. Nothing is enough. A decade of heat begging to be released.

"Please, Cooper. I need you."

I align myself and pause, cock nudging his entrance. Our eyes meet. "I love you, Jace."

I press into him. We both moan. He's so tight, gripping me so hard. His hands are on my hips, urging me closer—

Another moan.

Memories crash into me with every thrust. We're standing in the cave on our toes, arms wide, imagining what it would be like to fall into the stars.

Like this. It feels like this.

We're at Rainbow's End, sitting in the stern of a giant swinging ship. It rocks us so high I think we're going full circle. For a second, it hovers. Gravity steals my scream and tickles every inch of me senseless before slamming back into me as we fall.

I thrust again and again and again, and Jace lets out small pleasured grunts. He arches into me, head slamming against the pillow as if he's lost to everything but the love and the mounting pleasure between us.

I scratch along his arms and urge them upwards, where I knot our hands together. My hips swivel, my thrusts short and slow.

We are talking on the phone, one of our weekly conversations when he first moved. I am lying on his bed, the heel of my hand resting on my hard groin.

Then we are in the cave again, and I'm confessing my feelings for him.

As if he can read my mind, he lifts his head and catches my lips into a kiss. "Cooper!"

My name falling so deep and urgent from his lips spikes our passion toward climax. I take hold of his cock and stroke him in time to my thrusts. The build of his orgasm makes his ass clutch my cock. We ride the last waves as they peak, peak, peak—

"Jace!" I moan as my orgasm rushes over me, zipping from my groin to my fingertips. Jace lets out a cry and his body jerks. He spills warm come between us.

I collapse on top of him, his breath panting at my ear and tickling me into a shiver. Jace wraps his arms around me.

"Beautiful."

I shift to look at him. He's looking right back at me. No shame, no doubt, no question in his eyes.

Perhaps he sees one in mine, because he touches my cheek. "I'm sorry I was such a fool. I'm sorry I thought it had to matter. It doesn't. All I Want Is You."

pounamu

Pounamu—also known as nephrite, greenstone or jade—is a balancing stone used to ensure harmonious relationships.

Uplift and erosion bring these metamorphic stones to earth's surface. Heartbreak, loss, grief, friendships, family, and love have led me to this moment. Have brought me home.

Jace and I sit at the dining room table with Dad, Annie, and Mum, who we have invited over here.

Dad's brows furrow as he cradles one of Lila's favorite china teacups.

"We asked you here because we want to share something with you," I say carefully, glancing at Jace next to me.

He smiles at me, nervous but determined. We're on our balcony, staring at each other as flickering flames devour the envelope. "This is the truth," Jace says.

I glance at Mum and Annie, who give me a soft, understanding nod. They know what this is about. Annie gives me an encouraging smile, while Mum carefully lifts the teapot and refills Dad's cup.

"Share?" Dad says, looking between us. "What's that?"

Jace's Adam's apple juts out with a swallow. "Do you have those stones?"

I pull out the stones Jace asked me to bring downstairs, and I line them on the table.

Jace's lips twitch and he murmurs, "Already in chronological order."

I smile, rubbing his thigh under the table. He shifts nearer as if to absorb my strength.

He picks up the first stone, small and round. "The first stone I gave Cooper." He rolls it between his fingers. "This is when *we* began."

Dad frowns but doesn't say anything.

Jace picks up the blue lazurite, stone of universal truth and friendship. "This was the stone Cooper collected on my seventeenth birthday."

"You'll have to explain better," Dad says, and sips his tea. "I don't understand what exactly you're sharing." But his hands are shaking a bit, and I think maybe he's guessed after all.

Gently, Jace sets the blue lazurite down and gestures to the next stones: limestone, quartz, granite, amethyst, aquamarine, moonstone. "I gave these to Cooper, too."

I pinch his thigh, lean over and whisper, "Finally, you admit it!"

His cheeky grin makes it feel like he pinched *me*. "You knew. I knew you knew. It's always been that way." The spark of his smile ignites me deeply. "When I look at your stones, I remember." Jace glances over to Annie, Mum, and finally Dad. "I remember what each of these stones mean because I was with Cooper for a lot of them. Falling in love with him."

Dad draws in a deep breath. "I don't understand," he says. "You're brothers."

"Stepbrothers," Mum and Annie say together.

Dad opens his mouth and shakes his head. He presses his mouth into a thin line. "I understand this has been a stressful time for you boys. We do strange things when we grieve, but—"

I rise out of my seat. "No, Dad. This has been happening since the beginning. Since the divorce started. I love Jace."

"Are you sure it's love and you're not confusing it with—"

"Dad!" Jace's chair skids over the floor as he stands next to me. He takes my hand and links our fingers together. "Have you ever had that feeling of teetering at the edge of a precipice? Ever been so afraid to fall, even when falling is all you can dream of?

Ever looked at Mum and taken a steadying breath, not because she's holding you back from falling but because you know she'll catch you when you do?"

Dad hesitates and rubs his head. "I think I'm too tired."

"Answer us," I say quietly. "Please."

Dad looks at us, then at Mum and Annie, who are watching him carefully. He sinks back in his chair. "You know about this already."

"I suspected," Mum says, shifting so she's facing Dad.

"I didn't." Dad rubs his forehead as if he can smooth out the frown. "I don't."

"Sometimes love doesn't work out the way you hope it to." Mum smiles wonkily at Dad. "Sometimes, you think you're in love but you're not."

Her gaze shifts to Jace and me. "Sometimes you hope you're not but you are."

She laughs gently. "You don't get to choose your family, and you don't always get to choose who you fall in love with." Mum looks at Annie and back to Dad. "You may hate it and wish you could change it, but in the end, you have two choices: cut yourself off from everything or accept it and embrace it because love doesn't disappear."

Mum nods. "Our sons are always going to be welcome in my home."

Jace lets out a slow breath, and we both face Dad. Waiting. Hoping.

"How is it that you're only together now?" Dad says. "Why not then? Why not tell us—me—earlier?"

"Because I was a fool," Jace says. "Because I was scared of what you and others would think."

"And now you don't care what I think?"

"No," Jace says. I shake my head.

Jace carefully passes the stones back to me. I put them in my pocket and resume my seat. Before Jace sits, he pulls out five more stones from his pocket.

"What are these—?"

I try to touch them but Jace stops me, saying in my ear, “Let me explain first.”

He takes the first stone. “Germany, in an old town called Lubeck. A dropstone from the ice age.” He lifts my hand from his thigh and sets the stone on my palm. Then he picks up the next one. “France, Paris by the Seine.” The third. “Turkey at the Göreme Fairy Chimneys.”

It touches my palm, lurching me into the past where I am sitting with him at Lila and Dad’s wedding drinking whiskey. I know what the next stones are.

The fourth. “The Giant’s Causeway in Ireland.” The fifth, a bluestone like the one he got his mum. “And of course, Stonehenge.”

Jace closes my hand around them. “I have a hundred more I couldn’t bring back with me but they all represent the stupidest thing I’ve done: not taking you with me.”

Dad sighs. His teacup rattles against the saucer as he puts it down. He glances out toward the patio and the brightness outside.

“Your mother wrote me a letter, Jace. It took me a while to open it, and it was hard to read, some things I never knew and she never told me.” He shifts, glancing toward his tea. “She hinted that you two have a special love and she wants you both to be happy.” A few beats of silence. “Your mum is right. Love doesn’t just go away.” He stares at us, his expression growing stern. “I’m not turning my back.”

He pushes his chair back, and I call out, stones digging into my palms. “Dad?”

He walks toward the patio. Stops in front of it.

“We love you.”

He nods, then opens the doors and lets the sunshine in.

Mum follows after him, and Annie makes an excuse to leave the two of us alone.

I place Jace’s confession into my pocket. Bathed in light, Jace pivots his chair toward mine.

“Do you regret it?”

"Only that I didn't do it earlier." He stands, pulling me up with him. "Come."

I follow him upstairs to the gaming room. He leads me to the piano and pats the stool. "Sit next to me."

I raise a brow. "Going to play me another song?"

He shakes his head. "Well, maybe. After."

"After, what?"

He pulls a small black pouch from his pocket and opens the drawstring. "This is for you. I got it in Coober Pedy. You'll love it there."

He pulls out a small stone and presses it against my palm. It glitters all shades of color in the light.

Opal.

I hold it tightly, and I can't hold back anymore. I grab his T-shirt, hauling him against me. He twists around and straddles my lap, the weight of the greenstone hook under his T-shirt resting on my thumb.

"Are you offering to take me around the world? To Australia?"

He smirks. "What if I am?"

I laugh. "Would it just be travel?"

He kisses me. "What else would it be?"

epilogue

Music stirs in the air, pulling me out of my sleep. I turn over, sheets sliding silkily over my body. Jace's side of the bed is still warm. Though he said he'd try, I knew tonight would be too hard for him to sleep.

I crawl out of bed and pull on a pair of boxers that were puddled on the floor from earlier, when Jace grabbed me tightly and kissed me deeply. Afraid.

Afraid that I might not be there when he wakes up. *Don't leave me*, he whispered. Just as he had the night before his mum passed.

Three years ago now.

I walk the hall of our modest flat, opening to a living room that's dimly lit. Jace is at the piano playing his mum's melodies. I slide on the stool next to him and revel in the music vibrating around us. A prayer. Or perhaps, a conversation. Jace telling his mum about the things she missed this year: his first teaching job at Newtown High, my earning a doctorate in geology, us traveling to Stonehenge again like we did the first year after she passed.

The music grows softer. Gentle notes linger even after Jace has stopped.

He wraps his arms around me, kissing my neck. "Hey, beautiful. Sorry I woke you."

"Sorry I fell asleep."

The opal Jace gave me is set into a wristband, and it glows against my skin. I fiddle with it now as I think of something comforting to say to my man.

Jace smiles as if he knows exactly what I'm thinking. He touches the opal, rubbing his thumb over it.

"My favorite rock," I say.

"I know."

I shake my head, taking his hand and balling his fingers into a fist. I hold his fist tightly, like I did once a long time ago. I whisper, "Not the opal. You."

~ THE END ~

Acknowledgments

As always, thank you first to my wonderful husband for being supportive and not hesitating to entertain our son when I was riveted to writing a scene—or three.

Big hearty cheers to Natasha Snow for the cover art! I love how well it captures the mood and themes of the story. Thanks also for helping me come up with a more satisfying end to the story.

Teresa Crawford, thanks for helping me to structure this story, especially during those first developmental stages.

To editor Lynda Lamb, for going through and tweaking all those spelling errors and missing words, and for working me in your tight schedule while you were moving!

Thanks to HJS Editing for copyediting. Your edits helped to really tighten the narrative, and helped the story achieve a nice flow.

Another thanks to Vicki for reading and offering valuable feedback, and to Sunne for catching those inconsistencies. And big smiles to Maria and Mishyjo for test reading and catching final slip-ups.

Oh, and a shout out to Carolin, who listened to my story idea and worked me through some of the kinks.

16134932R00154

Made in the USA
San Bernardino, CA
19 October 2014